# CLAIMED BY THE KINGS

LOKI RENARD

Published by Stormy Night Publications and Design, LLC.
www.StormyNightPublications.com

Cover design by Korey Mae Johnson
www.koreymaejohnson.com

Images by Period Images, 123RF/Viacheslav Lopatin, and
123RF/magenta10

1st Print Edition. December 2016

ISBN-13: 978-1541002357

ISBN-10: 1541002350

# CHAPTER ONE

Feminine sobs filled a room swimming in wisps of smoke from the fires in the castle town below. Two tall masculine figures stood over Princess Elizabeth of Ammerdale, a beautiful young woman recently come of age whose hair was as red as the flames leaping near the ruins of the old castle gate.

"Don't cry, dear." A strong male hand descended gently on Elizabeth's red-gold locks. "All will be well."

The shivering, naked princess squeezed her eyes tightly shut and gasped a panicked little breath. There was good reason for her state; she had woken from a deep and dreamless sleep to find herself at the mercy of two dangerous men, each with an intimidating weapon drawn in the aftermath of battle. It would have been a perturbing discovery on its own had there not also been some... unpleasantness with her guards in the minutes following her waking. She was cowering on the floor having vacated her bed in an effort to flee, but there was no fleeing the force of fate.

King Milo Lionheart regretted the fact she had seen her personal guards wounded, but invasion was a nasty business at the best of times and they had refused to stand down even

1

though the rest of the castle had fallen. His men had taken those brave souls away to tend their wounds, leaving Princess Elizabeth vulnerable and alone with him and his unlikely companion.

"Stop pawing the girl," Ragnar barked gruffly. "We have yet to come to terms."

Milo rose to his feet, leaving Elizabeth sniveling at his boots as he faced his unexpected ally—and anticipated rival. They had both planted boots and flags in the very heart of Ammerdale, the Middle Kingdom. Where Milo reigned over the northern lands, Ragnar was the king of the southern kingdom, as far as those lawless lands full of rough barbarian men could ever be said to be ruled by a king.

The two men could not have been more different in aspect and temperament. Milo was famous for his height, his shock of bright blond hair, and his strategic ruthlessness in battles. He had bright blue intelligent eyes, a handsome face that held wisdom and strength in equal measure, and a body that had been hardened by battle, but that was naturally agile in form. He was a young king, five and twenty years old, but he was an able and ambitious one.

Ragnar preferred to go by his unofficial moniker: Ragnar the Barbarian. He never wore a crown, preferring instead the furs of his ancestors. He was brave and he was bold, a powerfully built man with prominent musculature that was evident in every part of his body. His jaw was square and strong, his shoulders were broad, his chest was like a muscular barrel and was visible under the leather harness to which his shield was still strapped against his back. He had eyes of such intense brown that they almost appeared black, ringed with long dark lashes that were matched by the black stubble of his beard, which was just starting to see a touch of gray as he approached his thirtieth year.

"She is close to catatonic with shock," Milo said to the barbarian. "There will be little to come to terms over if she is not clothed and fed."

"Who will clothe her?" Ragnar grunted.

"And who will feed her?" Milo asked the second question in turn. Truth be told, they were in a rather curious standoff. Elizabeth was the unfortunate princess of a kingdom they had conquered at much the same time. Both campaigns had come to a head at the capital city, which had fallen in record time thanks to assault from all sides. There was no sign of the king of Ammerdale, just his daughter sleeping sky-clad in her bed at the top of the tower in which Milo and Ragnar now stood facing one another in victory.

"I will." Their voices came in unison.

Milo let out a laugh at the situation the fates had put them in. "We have divided all the treasures and territories of this kingdom, but this one."

Ragnar snorted. "This one cannot be divided, only taken."

Both men fell momentarily silent, looking down at the girl whose life was at their mercy. Her pale curves and soft red flowing locks drew gazes of lust and pity. She was so completely vulnerable, and so entirely desirable. There was no doubt in Milo's mind that he was looking at the true crown jewel.

"I will trade you the gold reserves of the northern mines for her."

"No." The word fell heavily from Ragnar's lips. "You take the gold reserves. I'll have the princess."

Milo's brow rose. He was surprised that Ragnar was turning down gold. The man had a known obsession with riches; barbarians always did. They found power in the material. Milo's more educated caste understood more subtle forms of power. Ragnar was not stupid, but Milo expected him to be base in his desires as a general rule.

Milo's reasons for wanting to take the princess as his bride were many and complex. In addition to being very beautiful, Elizabeth would make a very useful wife. She was well bred, connected to the kingdoms to the east and the west and he was certain once she settled she would make a suitable partner as well. It was said she had a talent for

LOKI RENARD

poetry and dance, and had been tutored in foreign tongues. Ragnar would not have use for any of those things.

"If it is her body you desire, you could find many wenches with lustful forms," he said in an attempt to convince Ragnar to give up his claim to the princess.

Ragnar snorted again, looking at Milo with a dark gaze that Milo was starting to think did not lack as much intellect as he had previously imagined. There was a gleam in Ragnar's eyes that was more than simple sexual conquest.

"I want a son from her womb," he said bluntly. "She would do my bloodline proud. No amount of gold can buy strong progeny."

Their reasons were different, but equally compelling. Under other circumstances, the better brawler would have simply taken Elizabeth for his own, but there was no way either of them could steal the princess. They were at the end of a long campaign and both armies were fatigued and ready to celebrate victory together. Triumphant mingling was already taking place in the castle below.

"What do you want her for, pretty king?" Ragnar barked the question at him.

The jest made Milo's eyes narrow slightly. Ragnar was taunting him. Milo's handsome features earned him favor with women, and admiration among men, but Ragnar was the sort of barbarian who thought good looks were tantamount to weakness—though he should have known better, for they both stood triumphant in the same space. The irony of the jibe was that Ragnar was also a good-looking man, though perhaps in a simpler, rougher way.

"She bears the blood of all four directions," Milo said simply. "Whoever has her, has the ear of the continent's courts."

A derisive snort emanated from the barbarian. "A beautiful woman, and all you can think of is politics."

"A political coup at your feet, and all you can think of is rutting," Milo rejoined. "You are a walking cock."

Now they were even in their jibes.

4

It was Elizabeth who settled the argument. Having laid practically silent aside from sobbing, and offered no resistance at all from the moment her bedchamber was breached, she suddenly came to life, much like a striking snake.

A blade appeared in her hand, likely having been secreted under the pillow she had been clutching for security. She lashed out at Milo and almost caught his boot with the sharp edge of the dagger. He jumped back a step and let out a cry of surprise. Ragnar laughed heartily at Milo's shock, slapping his knee with raucous humor.

"She is too bold for you, pretty king."

Milo cut his eyes at Ragnar. "Call me pretty king but once more and I…"

The princess slashed at him again, forcing him to once more evade her threat.

Ragnar's laughter grew louder as the naked young woman squirmed around, her blade aimed at Milo, who was still much closer than Ragnar was—at least until the barbarian took one large step forward, reached down and wrapped his large hand around her ankle.

"I will save you, pretty… ho there!"

In an instant, Elizabeth had curled up on herself and stabbed the knife toward his hand, forcing him to let her go.

It was Milo's turn to laugh at the bewildered expression on Ragnar's face. He hadn't expected her to attack him too, so it seemed.

"Too bold for your blood too," he chortled.

They both stood back, looking down at their prisoner whose breasts and bright red flare of fur between her thighs were visible now that she had rolled onto her back and was holding the dagger in two hands.

There was a fierceness to her beauty now, but no real danger. She was like a spitting wild kitten, capable of sinking needle-sharp claws into a hand or finger and causing pain, but nothing resembling a match for the power of either of the men standing over her.

"Now, princess," Milo censured her gently. "Put the knife down. We mean you no harm."

Her lips parted and she spoke the first words she had uttered since their joint invasion. "Go boil your head."

A snort from Ragnar drew her furious green eyes in his direction. "Rebellious wench," he growled. "A good dose of the flat of my hand will settle her."

Milo was inclined to agree. Elizabeth was young and impulsive. Discipline was important for high-spirited ladies of good breeding. She had doubtless been spoiled in her formative years. Her kingdom was a small, but rich one. Her father's father had been a prince from the eastern kingdom, her mother a famously beautiful princess from the west. That made Elizabeth a central figure in a great many respects, spoiled and feted by three kingdoms.

Though ostensibly the invasion had been about expanding his lands and holdings, Milo had made his journey in large part for Princess Elizabeth. He was beginning to think that Ragnar had made the very same decision. Milo had ridden out from his home on the day of her eighteen birthday. It seemed likely that Ragnar had begun his invasion at much the same time. They had been in a race for conquest of more than mere territory, and now their quarry was between them, in reach and yet very much not in reach.

"I will sell my life dearly," Elizabeth declared bravely.

"That won't be necessary, darling," Milo drawled calmly. "We'd both rather you kept it."

"Put the knife down. Now." Ragnar growled the order in a tone that commanded obedience.

Elizabeth kept her hands wrapped around the dagger, her eyes darting between them as her pale, perfect breasts rose and fell with every breath she took. Even in her resistance, she was beautifully fragile.

•••••••

She had thought it must be a dream when two large men appeared in her chamber. Elizabeth still wasn't sure. She could feel the floor at her back and the hilt of the ornate blade in her hands. They both felt real, but dreams could be vivid and surely there could not be two kings of opposing kingdoms arguing over her in the middle of the night? Had the war truly come so close to home? It had been raging on many fronts for quite some time. She had been cloistered away for several months in the tower, restricted to activities such as sewing and singing, and her father had forbidden any news be given to her. He did not want her to worry about such things, so he said. Some of her maids had whispered little bits and pieces to her, but she had never known quite what to believe.

Now she did not know if she could believe her own eyes—though she recognized both men from the tales that were widely told about them. The tall one could be no other than King Milo Lionheart. He wore the sigil of a rampant winged lion upon his chest and he was just as handsome as was told of in the songs the bards sang. If they had met under more refined circumstances, she would have been very pleased to make his acquaintance.

She met his blue gaze, saw in it desire and some good humor. It was enough to make her clench her thighs together, both to preserve what was left of her modesty and to hide the way her nethers were responding.

Her eyes darted from Milo to the other man, King Ragnar. She would have wanted her dagger at her side regardless of the time and place of their meeting. He had an air of rough danger that was palpable and he made her quiver in quite a different way than Milo. Now she met his dark gaze, she felt her body responding yet again. It was a forceful, primal reaction that had nothing to do with sense and everything to do with her animal form.

"You are being rather naughty, princess," Milo purred. "Put down the knife and save more unnecessary unpleasantness."

It was difficult to keep her eyes on both men, standing as they were on either side of her. Escape was impossible. She knew that she would be taken. She should lower her knife and accept her fate, but she could not. The excitement and the fear were far too great. Both these men, these proud kings were looking at her with a carnal hunger that made every part of her tremble.

She saw a glance pass between them a moment before Milo leaned toward her again. She swiped at him with the knife, a motion that made her roll toward him. In that moment of exposure, Ragnar's hard hand came down across her bottom in a slap that sent a sudden shock through her body and a flash of heat across her cheeks. It was enough to make her grip on the knife loosen, and to distract her so that Milo could pluck the hilt of it from her hands, neatly disarming her.

He smiled down at her with warm triumph as her hands went back to cover her now stinging bottom.

"You are fools," she hissed angrily, fear rising strongly as she realized she was now totally at their mercy. "A pretty boy and a bandit. I will not be had by either one of you."

Milo shook his head at her, blond strands of hair falling into his piercing eyes for a moment before he pushed them back. "Now, princess," he said in his cultured tones. "Be a good girl and mind your tongue."

"I will not be a good girl, and certainly not for you," she threw back rebelliously. "I was not raised to be some meek woman as you have in your countries, too afraid to speak or show themselves in the light of day. The blood of four royal houses runs in my veins. I…"

Her proud speech was cut short as the barbarian behind her sat down on the bed, took hold of her by the upper arm, and unceremoniously pulled her up from the floor and then over his lap. She found her naked body pressed against his leather-clad thighs and his iron slab abdominal plane. He had no pretty words for her. Instead his palm met her bare bottom as he started to spank her.

"What are you doing!?" She made the inquiry at the top of her lungs. Elizabeth had never been punished in her life. Being struck by the barbarian king was not only painful and embarrassing, it was utterly confusing. The physical sensations were powerful, a heat searing through her skin, making it feel hot and tight and an ache in the flesh below, the muscle of her bottom contracting sharply with every single slap.

"You pulled a blade," Ragnar growled. "And you have an insolent tongue. This is punishment for both sins."

Elizabeth struggled to free herself, but he seemed to be infinitely powerful. Her naked form was no match for his muscle. He clamped an arm about her waist and she was locked in place, her legs flailing as she kicked and squirmed furiously.

"Unhand me, brute!"

Her words were met with a slap to her upper thigh. Elizabeth let out a shriek. She had not known that it was possible to feel such a sudden sharp bolt of pain. It was as though she could feel each place his fingers had landed individually.

"You are tender, princess," Ragnar said, his large rough hand passing over her bottom and thigh, rubbing the spot he had spanked. "You skin is soft and your flesh is unaccustomed to chastisement. You should be more careful of what comes out of your mouth."

She let out a sound somewhere between a growl and a whimper. It was most frustrating and humbling to be pinned against the body of a powerful man who was insisting she show him respect and deference though he was nothing but a brutish invader.

He spanked her until the heat grew so great she was certain her bottom was swollen beyond all measure. Her body had ceased to be hers and only responded to him; his touch, the slaps of his hard hand, which set a rhythm that felt more primal than her own heartbeat. Her hips jolted with it, the hard little bud that usually hid in the folds of her womanhood becoming erect and grazing against his thigh with every single slap.

She was aware of Milo's eyes on her. It would have been bad enough to have been spanked by a barbarian king, but to know she was under a debonair blue gaze, to be made to feel so very small and so very naughty made her feel thoroughly chastised.

Did he know? There was something in his eyes when she glanced at him briefly through her cascading hair that told her that she could have little in the way of secrets from such a man. It was difficult to put coherent thoughts together when her bare form was still being so thoroughly punished by the barbarian.

The liquid trickling between her lower lips was a concern. She had felt herself become damp before when gazing at particularly stimulating men, but she had never been this wet. It was as though some wicked imp had turned a pump on between her thighs and made desire flow from the very core of her.

As she had feared, the barbarian did not take long to notice her shameful condition. His hand slid from her hot bottom between her thighs. With little in the way of ceremony he pushed them apart and put her feminine mound on display, his fingers cupping her pussy.

"Look at her," Ragnar said, his fingers holding her lower lips spread wide. "She is dewy as a lily on a spring morning."

Elizabeth's mouth parted in a gasp as he used the index finger of his other hand to stroke the insides of her lips, not quite penetrating her womanhood, but caressing it softly. He looked up at Milo with a wicked, carnal smile.

"What would you give to sink inside this pink heaven?"

• • • • • • •

In that moment, Milo would have given almost anything. His cock was like diamond and had been from the moment her reddened bottom had begun to bounce over Ragnar's thighs. She was utterly exquisite, from her soft pale lips surrounded by soft reddish curls, to the inner aperture of her pussy. Ragnar had her inner lips spread so Milo could see the little thin barrier of hymen just past the entrance of her body.

Animal instinct was taking over, and soon all three of them would be beyond the sway of sense and reason.

"Give her to me," Milo said. "And I will give you these lands. All of them."

Ragnar chuckled softly and shook his head. "Lands must be defended. Subjects must be ruled. This one…" He palmed her bottom with his other hand and slapped her cheek lightly. "This is the only thing I am interested in conquering."

Milo held back a growl. Every masculine impulse he had was telling him to draw his sword, run the barbarian through, and take Elizabeth for his own. He knew Ragnar had the same instincts. It was a credit to them both that they resisted those baser desires.

"There can be only one solution to this," he said, using the last of his mental powers. "We must…"

"…share her," Ragnar finished his sentence.

"Share her," Milo agreed.

Elizabeth began to squirm again at hearing their decision, but Ragnar did not allow her even a moment of anything other than complete submission.

"She is more trouble than one man," the barbarian said as he pinned her harder against his thighs and swatted her bottom harshly. "Stay!" He barked the order down at her.

She settled into sullen stillness, but for her hips, which could not seem to help their tantalizing dance.

"If we are to share her… who is to take her first?"

Ragnar let her lower lips close and rubbed his broad hand over her reddish mound. "I have little use for a virgin," he smirked. "I do not think she will like being broken in by me. Your cock is more suited to novices, I am sure."

It was a jibe that Milo was content to let pass without

answer. He was not concerned about his endowment, only that the princess should feel his cock inside her first, that he should be the one to teach her what it was to be a woman in the arms of a man.

"Put her on the bed," he said. "We will seal this now with blood and seed."

Ragnar slid Elizabeth off his lap, adjusting her on the bed as if she were little more than a plaything. He was so much larger and stronger than her that resistance was utterly impossible. Where his large hands put her, she was forced to stay, lying upon her back between two strong men. To ensure there was not any further resistance from the young lady, Ragnar took a handful of hair under the back of her head and held her there as Milo put his hands to his waist and began to undo his belt.

This was a moment of trust between him and Ragnar. He would be caught with his pants down. If Ragnar was setting a trap for him, he was about to fall into it. Elizabeth's red bottom drew his gaze and his mind; the curve of her hot cheeks and the wet gleaming red furred slit between them chased much of Milo's customary caution out of his mind.

He did not remove any more of his armor than was necessary to free his cock, which sprung out thick and hard between the base of his mail shirt and the upper part of his leggings, which he had parted for the purpose.

"Let her go," he instructed. "She will beg for this before she receives it."

Ragnar snorted and stood up, moving to stand several paces away on the other side of the bed, his arms folded across his chest in a show of relative safety. If he were to try to attack, Milo would have ample time to respond.

Milo had no time to be concerned with Ragnar. His attention was locked on Elizabeth as she lay there looking up at him with an uncertain but lustful expression. At eighteen years of age, Elizabeth was more than primed for a man. Her virtue was famous. Though some suitors had tried to take her earlier, her father had been vicious in protecting her virginity. There were very unpleasant tales about what had happened to men who had pursued her in the past.

The King of Ammerdale was not there that night, however, and Elizabeth's virginal womanhood was glistening with need. Milo could scent her arousal as he leaned down and knelt upon the bed, moving to lay beside her. This was not how he had imagined his first time with the princess, but he was as much a slave to the whims of fate as she was.

He pressed his lips to hers and felt her uncertainty there in the kiss. She was trembling, perhaps out of excitement, perhaps out of fear. He slid his arm around her, his large hand circling around the small of her back as he began to kiss her with a slow passion. She was hesitant at first as his tongue slid into her mouth and began to massage hers, but after a few moments she started to respond. Her mouth opened wider and her body began to melt against his, her soft breasts meeting the hard plane of his chain mail-clad body.

Milo cupped her ass, his cock stiffening all the more as she moaned into his mouth along with a little squeak of discomfort. He was sure her bottom was sore, Ragnar had been quite stern with her—and she had earned and needed every bit of it. Milo let his hand run over her cheeks as he continued to kiss her, feeling her relax more, start to moan as her hips began to move in a feminine gyration that was common to every aroused female from the lowliest bar wench to the most well-bred princess.

He lifted his mouth from hers, slid down between her thighs, and pressed his lips against her core.

"Oh!" Her feminine cry of surprise brought a dark chuckle from Ragnar.

Milo flashed a grin at both Elizabeth and Ragnar as his mouth settled on the petals of her pussy, his tongue teasing the folds to swollen life. She was wet, but he wanted to initiate her the right way. He wanted her to feel the pleasure

13

of a man's mouth on her quim before he split her with his rod.

She tasted most delicious, he discovered as the tip of his tongue not only traced the folds of her sex, but dipped deeper as well into the welling chalice between her inner lips. Elizabeth began to moan and buck her hips so forcefully that he clamped them between his hands and held her there upon his lips and tongue, working his gentle mouth magic upon her until she cried out with ecstasy and he felt a fresh flow of arousal running from deep within her.

He glanced over the pale writhing form of her body and saw lust written on Ragnar's face. The barbarian's eyes were locked on her face, which was flushed with pure arousal. She was looking back at the barbarian, her head tipped back, her chest pressed upward, tight nipples erect in the cool air.

Milo could resist no longer. It was a swift seduction by all parties as he slid up her body and pressed his cock to the entrance of her lips, leaving the thick head of it just outside the tight tunnel. Elizabeth let out another gasp and now her eyes were on him, bright sparkling green gaze locking with his as he held himself still with all the discipline he had in his body.

"Tell me what you want, princess," he teased. "Would you have this cock inside you?"

His hands were no longer holding her hips in place so she was free to wriggle and writhe. She did both, her wet lower lips spreading her desire over the head of his manhood, coating his glans with hot desire. He could have plunged deep into her at any moment, ripped through her hymen and satisfied himself at her expense, but he wanted to see the desperation in her eyes reach an even higher peak. He wanted to hear her sweet voice beg him.

"…please." The word came so softly in between gasps that it was barely audible.

"Please what, princess?" He took hold of his rod in one hand and ran the hot head of it around the gleaming bud of her clit, rubbing around and around the tight little nub until

Elizabeth could stand it no longer.

"Please put… it inside me…" She blushed so furiously, the hue of her face almost matched that of her hair.

The request was a very virginal one. She could not bring herself to so much as mouth the word cock, or even a more delicate term for his manhood, but there was no doubt that she wanted Milo's rod with every part of her being. He slid it slowly down her slit, finding the dewy entrance once more. An expression of anticipation and perhaps even a little fear passed over her beautiful face. She was on the precipice of a transformation from maiden to woman and she did not know what it would bring. Elizabeth was beautiful, but she was so vulnerably desirable in that moment that Milo could not have held back even had he wanted to. His cock yearned to be buried inside her hot, tight chalice, to take the first strokes inside her virginal quim.

He eased forward, the flared head of his cock parting her soft, wet lips, slowly sinking into the uncharted territory of her oh so hot, clenching pussy. She let out a soft breath as his cock finally slid inside her, her body welcoming him with a wet embrace. The thin barrier of her hymen put up little resistance as he pushed forward in one firm stroke.

Milo saw her wince as the barrier gave way. It must have caused her some small measure of discomfort, but probably no more than the thrashing Ragnar had given her bottom. She certainly did not seem to want him to stop. Her hands reached for him, grasped his arms, and again he regretted the circumstances of their coupling for she could only take hold of chain mail and not feel any part of him besides the thick, hard flesh spearing deep inside her.

"To hell with it," he growled, reaching down to his mail shirt. He pulled it up and over his head, baring his upper body in one decisive motion that left his torso bare to both Elizabeth and Ragnar. The barbarian could have him now with a single swing of his hefty axe, but Milo didn't care. He wanted to feel her sweet body against his, her fingers on his skin, her soft breasts pressed against his chest as he laid himself over her and joined fully with her in slow strokes, his hips rolling with each and every thrust so every part of her tight, no longer virginal channel was pleasured.

Though she had been a virgin, there was no doubt that the princess had the orgasmic instincts of a highly sexed woman. As Milo made love to her, she clung to him for dear life, as if she were drowning in a sea of sensation. He felt every quiver and tremor in her body as though it were his body. They were joined so deeply he was almost certain they were one being; she moved with him as if she had made love to him many times before. Her innocence was still in her eyes, but there was nothing innocent about the way her hips gyrated and made her cunt dance around his cock, grinding in a slow, intense motion that made the cum roil in his balls.

He held back from the point of climax, wanting her to reach orgasm again. He was mindful of the barbarian still looking on. The man's lust would have to be sated and Milo doubted Ragnar would spare Elizabeth another round. He would want to claim her cunt, and he would likely do it in a rough and untamed fashion.

With that in mind, Milo took hold of her firmly and rolled over so that she was atop him. Elizabeth let out a little squeal of surprise, her lips parting in a smile as she found herself looking down at him through a curtain of red hair. There was a brief moment of privacy in that moment, just the two of them locking eyes behind the red shades.

And then she tossed her head and ground herself against him, forcing her pussy down as deep on his cock as it would go and Milo groaned with the effort it took not to fill her then and there. She was a natural sybarite, a sexual siren who called to every part of him. Looking up at her, the curves of hip and breast accentuated by the position, he was in total thrall to her beauty.

She began to slide up and down his shaft, following the instincts and desires of her body. Milo knew it was a matter of strokes before he lost the battle with his orgasm, so he reached around her with both hands and spread her bottom cheeks. Her lubrication was flowing between her thighs and it was a simple matter to scoop a little of the warm viscous liquid with his middle and index finger and rub it against the bud of her anus.

She jerked against him, her green eyes flying wide open as he curled his fingers against the sensitive spot, locking her between his cock and his fingers. She could not grind any deeper against him, and moving back would mean pushing her bottom onto his digits.

Milo chuckled softly as Elizabeth whimpered adorably. He could feel her inner walls clutching him harder still and knew that he was having the desired effect. A hot blush was cascading over her body, a pink that rushed across her cheeks and the bridge of her nose, and over her breasts. Her breath came faster, a soft panting that brought with it a feminine moan that rose to a peak as she impaled herself hard against his cock and orgasmed profusely, her juices soaking his shaft as her nubile young body writhed atop him.

He could no longer hold back. His cum shot forth like a geyser, drawing a shout from him as it splashed deep inside Elizabeth, filling her tight cunt all the way to the brim until his seed came dripping out around his cock and he felt the warmth of his juices and hers combined upon his abdomen.

• • • • • •

Elizabeth slid from Milo, panting, but she was not yet done. One hungry, lustful word came from her mouth, her beautiful green eyes sparkling with an otherworldly elegance as she intoned her desire.

"More." Her tongue extended a little way and she licked her lips, her eyes locked on the second man. Milo watched with fascination as she extended a finger and crooked it toward the barbarian. Though she had been a virgin not minutes ago, her transformation into a sexual creature had been instantaneous. She was hungry for sensation, for pleasure, for men.

The barbarian was looming nearer. He seemed more dangerous than King Milo, and she was rather glad that Milo was still there. He was a moderating influence, a promise of some kind of safety as Ragnar began to discard his clothing. Unlike Milo, he did not go by half measures. He took the leather and furs and threw them from his body, revealing a broad, bulky form trammeled with muscle and scars from battles past. His skin was darker than Milo's, both from having a natural olive hue from the southern climes and also from exposure to the sun that had beaten down on him.

When he removed his belt and his loin covering, Elizabeth saw the thick rampant length of his cock hard against his belly. There was thick dark hair curling about the base of it, two heavy balls swinging between his legs.

Her eyes grew wide as the phallic beast drew closer, capturing her attention. She found herself leaning back against Milo for some kind of reassurance, though it was not so much fear that made the butterflies in her belly take flight, but anticipation.

She spread her legs and gazed up at him with lustful eyes. Ragnar required no more invitation. He entered her with no fanfare, taking his rightful place deep inside her.

Elizabeth lay back upon the bed in elegant feminine surrender to carnal pleasure as the barbarian began to fuck her, his hands on her thighs pulling her on and off his cock. Milo rolled to the side and caressed her as she was taken by the second king, her cunt lips wrapped tight around his thick shaft as Ragnar worked her back and forth again and again. He sat back on his knees, his thighs creating an inclined plane that her spanked bottom slid across as he took total control of her body.

It felt to Elizabeth as if she were in another world, as if the two men had transported her, transposed her, transmogrified her. Rocked back and forth against Ragnar's thick manhood, she moaned and writhed, her head falling back against the bed, her mouth kissed most thoroughly by Milo as her loins clenched and grasped at the thick root between them.

A second dose of seed was due to her, of that her body was absolutely certain. Ragnar leaned forward, spread her legs about his powerful hips and began to plunge harder inside her. She could feel his thick cock ravaging her tender walls, the last remnants of even the notion of virginity falling away under the pounding fury of his desire.

Such an erotic onslaught would have frightened her if she had not known Milo first, but in her heightened state of arousal born of having been filled with King Lionheart's seed, she welcomed Ragnar's rough animal desire, her hands clutching at his shoulders, her pale thighs wrapping around his waist as she lifted herself to him, their mouths meeting in frenzied kisses as the barbarian conquered her completely.

Elizabeth felt herself flying through sensations that crashed about her body, muscles tensing, quivering, burning for release. Ragnar's rough approach to climax was an elemental experience that obliterated her consciousness for an ecstatic moment as a second orgasm powered through her body, accompanied by another flooding of seed. The barbarian held her tightly, his long thick cock locked deep inside her as it pulsed every drop in his balls deep into her welling wet chalice.

When they separated, she felt strangely bereft. She was glad when both Milo and Ragnar laid on either side of her, recovering their breath and senses for what lay ahead. Though they were still strangers to her mind, they were no longer strangers to her body. Elizabeth lay in her bed with their cum slowly trickling between her swollen lower lips, feeling more sated than she had known it was possible to feel. It was as though she had been starving for years, but not known it, and now she was fed.

# CHAPTER TWO

In the aftermath of a coupling that left Milo quite drained and suddenly aware of the strangeness of his conquest, he became aware that Elizabeth had not once cried out for her father. She seemed to know that the king was not at hand. Where was the King of Ammerdale? Perhaps Ragnar had done away with the monarch in his campaign, but if he had, the news had not traveled to Milo.

Elizabeth was lying curled with a small smirk of satisfaction on her pretty face. She did not look conquered in that moment. She looked sated and—if such a thing were possible in such circumstances—spoiled.

Milo ran his fingers through her hair, brushing bright strands from her face. "I must ask you," he said. "You have not asked us what fate befell your father. Are you not curious?"

Elizabeth's pretty brow rose at him. "I would have thought you would be the curious one," she said. "Curious never to have met him in battle..."

"We thought he was fighting at the other front," Ragnar said gruffly, rising to his elbow.

"And we the same," Milo nodded.

"My father has been dead for three months," Elizabeth

said. "He was scratched by a stray blade and contracted an infection from which he did not recover. His generals have been commanding his armies." Her expression transformed from one of sadness to one of immense pride as the next words fell from her lips. "Trust and believe, if my father were alive, neither of you would have made it within a hundred miles of this place. He held the four borders for decades. Several lesser men were not able to do what he could alone."

Milo and Ragnar exchanged significant looks. That explained rather a lot. The resistance to their invasions had weakened considerably the closer they got to the capital. At least, that had been Milo's experience, and he strongly suspected it had been the same for Ragnar.

He rose from the bed, went to the bathing chamber adjoining her rooms, and took water and a cloth in a basin that had been left to stand. He returned to where Elizabeth was still lying upon the bed and began to sponge over her thighs and between her legs, washing her cum-covered mound with gentle strokes.

Ragnar watched dispassionately as he pulled his clothing back on. His axe was propped up against the wall, within arm's reach. Milo's weapon was beside the bed. Ragnar did not seem eager to rearm himself, which Milo was immensely grateful for. If they were to have any chance at an alliance, they would have to trust one another.

He turned his attention back to Elizabeth and sponged her thighs down gently, cleaning her mound of seed and sweat alike. She let out little moans as he took care of her most intimately, ensuring that no traces were left on her skin, aside perhaps from what was still trickling between her swollen lower lips.

"Pick your prettiest gown, princess," he said once she was relatively clean. "We have an appearance to make."

· · · · · · ·

21

Elizabeth had become a woman. She had always known she was female of course, but until the closed aperture of her chalice had been pierced by a man she had not guessed at the potential of her erotic response. Many nights she had furtively rubbed the little bud between her thighs and achieved a blush of relief, but that was nothing compared to the torrent of sensation the two kings had sent rushing through her with the thrusting of their rampant cocks.

Though she felt some rebellion in the manner of her taking, Elizabeth had been raised in the knowledge that one day she would be given to a king—or that one would take her. Her father had often bemoaned the fact that she was not a male child, not only because there was no heir to the throne, but because he knew the fates that befell beautiful princesses.

*Male or female, both fall to the sword*, he had often said, meaning a very different sword in the case of a princess than a prince. Elizabeth had always blushed when he said such things, not that he ever addressed them directly to her. It was usually something she overheard when he was speaking with his advisers. Elizabeth did have a habit of sneaking about to find out what was happening in the castle. She had to. People hid the truth of things from her all too often, and the maids and ladies in waiting would sometimes lie directly to her face. She had discovered that there was no truth but that which she experienced directly.

"Princess," Milo said, interrupting her reverie. "Do you have a preference?"

He was at her wardrobe, flicking through her dresses with what looked to Elizabeth with a practiced hand.

"Which is your favorite, pretty king? Will any of them fit you?" Ragnar mocked him in brutish tones, his words making Elizabeth giggle.

Milo turned and flashed an unrepentant grin. "I enjoy the sight of a beautiful woman in a beautiful gown," he said, pulling an emerald green satin dress from among the many in the wardrobe. It was one of Elizabeth's favorites, for the way it highlighted her eyes and made her hair gleam. "You are more used to bedding down with men, I understand," he taunted Ragnar right back.

Ragnar growled under his breath, but made no further comment. It seemed King Lionheart had won the skirmish of jests.

In addition to choosing her clothing, Milo was even so kind as to help her don the dress. It was quite impossible to lace herself into it, but he handled the strands with adept fingers, cinching the bodice tightly enough to fit her nicely, but not so tight that her breath was compromised.

"I helped my older sisters when they had lace emergencies," he explained in response to her astounded expression. "There are occasions on which a girl, having removed her dress, needs it to be restored to its former place without gossiping tongues wagging."

Ragnar snorted, but held his tongue. The inference was obviously that Milo's older sisters had been rather wayward and certainly not virginal upon their weddings. Elizabeth had heard the rumors too. Courtly gossip traveled far and wide and was most eagerly received in every castle in the land. She knew that Milo was from an elegant and progressive court. All of her finest fashions came from the seamstresses of the north. In fact, the very dress she was now wearing was from the north.

Once she was ready, Milo and Ragnar escorted her down to the castle proper. It was very strange to be ushered through the only home she'd ever known and to somehow view it through the eyes of a newcomer. The most familiar things suddenly seemed very different with two new forces occupying much of the castle and fortress.

Elizabeth had certainly never seen the great hall so full before. Two armies were mixed; Milo's knights with their gleaming armor and Ragnar's warriors in their leather and furs. She was not surprised to find that the last dregs of what had been her father's forces had fled, or as he would have put it, strategically retreated.

The rowdy men quietened down as Milo and Ragnar entered the hall with Elizabeth between them. A sudden tension entered the air, as the celebrating armies were confronted with the same dilemma that had been presented to Milo and Ragnar an hour earlier.

"Listen!" Ragnar roared over the straggling voices. "What you are about to hear may be the most important thing you ever hear, so open your ears and pay attention, brutes!"

Ragnar's barbarians fell silent along with Milo's soldiers and looked expectantly at the kings. It was Milo who ultimately made the announcement.

"When two armies meet, battle is usually imminent. Not tonight! Tonight Ragnar and I have forged a new alliance between our kingdoms. Some of you are loyal to the south. Others to the north. But now you have a new kingdom to be loyal to, a single great kingdom spanning from the very tip of the north to the very depths of the south. From sea to sea, we declare three kingdoms as one and Ammerdale City will be our new capital. You are two armies, but you will become one. We have a large territory to defend and new prospects to the east and west. There will be no north, no south. There will be only the Central Kingdom, the Middle Lands."

There was a moment of pregnant silence as he finished speaking. The news he had given was tremendous and unprecedented.

"To the Middle Lands!" Ragnar raised his voice and his fist, breaking the last of the tension.

A roar of approval came from the throats of the assembled soldiers. After a long campaign, a victory such as this one was a grand morale boost. They had made history and redrawn the borders of their lands. There could be no greater honor for a soldier.

Amid the chaos, Elizabeth instinctively retreated toward Milo. He was the more familiar of the two men. He was the one who seemed most like her and seemed the most inclined to be kind. Ragnar had not been cruel, but he cut a far more intimidating figure, which was amplified by the way he interacted with his men. The barbarians were a loud and lusty lot and they seemed much more familiar with Ragnar than Milo's soldiers did. Milo's men maintained a distance and respect, even in their revelry, which allowed Elizabeth some breathing room.

The kings took their seats at the head table, which was upon a raised dais at the head of the hall. Elizabeth had eaten many times at her father's side, usually at much smaller gatherings. Instead of sitting on her own chair, she allowed herself to be drawn into Milo's lap.

Mead, wine, and beer flowed plentifully from the castle's cellars, and pheasant and boar soon graced the long tables, gravy and bread filling the bellies of two famished armies. The celebration bought the men together and by the end of the evening, Milo's soldiers were wearing the bearskins of their new brothers in arms, and Ragnar's barbarians were drunkenly strutting about in pieces of shined armor.

"Wine, princess?" Milo held a chalice to her lips for her to sip.

He was looking after her as if she were a prized possession. She had not picked up a fork, or put food to her own mouth, but he had ensured that she both ate and drank. Elizabeth rather liked being taken care of in such a fashion; it was a comfort given the intense strangeness of the scene. The last time she had taken a meal in the great hall, her father had been alive and Ammerdale was regarded as being one of the most stable kingdoms in all the lands. Now it had fallen to two foes and she was the captive of not one, but two kings.

Strange that she should take comfort in her captor, but who else was there? Her guards were wounded and would likely be killed if they attempted any kind of rescue—and what kind of rescue could there be? Where could she go that she would not yet again find herself at the mercy of a man with a crown upon his head?

"Are you always so quiet, princess?" Milo asked the question in rather fond tones, but the question still made her bristle.

"Yes, I am always this quiet when two men destroy my family's legacy."

"Hardly," Milo said, running his hand over her rump. "You are still upon the throne, in a manner of speaking. If you think of it, this is the best possible outcome for your family's legacy. Ammerdale is now the center of a vast kingdom the likes of which your father could not have dreamed of."

Elizabeth narrowed her eyes, taking the comment about her father as something of a jibe. "We will see," she said. "Your alliance is an uneasy one. The barbarian is stronger than you are and his patience need only be as long as his arm and axe."

"Do not worry about my strength, princess," Milo said, utterly unperturbed by her comments. "Or the alliance. You will be well taken care of no matter what fate has in store for us. A princess always has value."

"I had value," she said. "Until you stripped me of my virtue and passed me between the two of you like a common… toy."

Milo tipped her head up to look at him. "As I recall, you were not so much passed around as allowed to spend yourself on two rods," he reminded her. "You are a lusty little wench, princess. I assure you, your value is untainted."

She blushed as she met his eyes. It was a difficult conversation to have and simultaneously maintain dignity. She could not look at him without remembering how it felt to have him deep inside her, piercing her hymen, taking her for the very first time. His seed was still seeping from her, she was sure of it. In spite of the tender cleaning he had bestowed on her, she had been very full with two loads of royal seed mixing deep inside her.

· · · · · · ·

Milo had Elizabeth curled up on his lap, the poor girl desperate for some comfort, Ragnar figured. She looked thoroughly exhausted and pale, her eyes closed against the raucous merriment of the evening. Milo was holding her in gentlemanly fashion, one arm about her shoulders, the other around her waist, shielding her from the fears she was curled up against.

Ragnar sat apart from Milo and Elizabeth, the least liquor-infused man in the room by a good measure. In spite of the reputation of his people, and the stories that followed him personally from place to place, Ragnar was not as impetuous or as wild as his appearance made others believe. He was powerful and battle hardened, however, and he was not sure he could say the same about his new ally.

Milo was younger than he by several years, full of enthusiasm and bravado, undoubtedly intelligent but a little too smart for his own good besides. Ragnar did not like to share, but the learned king from the north had made a good case for an alliance. Even if Ragnar had not been inclined to agree, his men were battle weary, and killing Milo would have started a war they were ill-prepared for. Resources were running low and a victory had to be declared lest a loss be sustained.

In spite of the pretty words, and the celebrations unfolding all around them, this alliance was an uneasy one for Ragnar. He did not know how long it would last, or who would break it, but it seemed to him that whichever one broke it first would be at the greatest advantage.

It was tempting to take his sword and run Milo through there in his chair.

He felt eyes on him and glanced over to see the princess Elizabeth looking at him with what could only be described as a calculating expression on her face. Another smart one. Ragnar snorted softly to himself and cocked his head to the side, meeting and assessing her gaze.

Her face was pressed against Milo's shoulder, her

expression hidden by the red-gold fall of her hair to everyone but him. Her green eyes held a wicked expression, reminding Ragnar that this was the daughter of three kingdoms. As vulnerable as she appeared to be, there was powerful blood in her veins.

His cock twitched in response to the challenge in her gaze. Seeing her in another man's arms made his baser instincts rise—jealousy, possessiveness. He quelled both of them in order to maintain the semblance of restraint he needed to keep the peace. Both Milo and Elizabeth would feel his reckoning soon enough.

# CHAPTER THREE

Elizabeth could no longer keep her eyes open, and after discussion with Ragnar, Milo decided to take her to bed. The revelry would not end that evening, of that he was sure, but the princess could not be expected to attend the full length of the celebrations, nor was it entirely appropriate that she do so. Just as he swept her sleepy form into his arms, he saw that many of the women from the castle town had made their way into the great hall somehow and were consuming liberal amounts of food and wine alongside the men. They came in less than modest dress, bosoms proudly displayed in dresses that left little to the imagination and that earned them the lascivious attentions of barbarians and soldiers alike.

In the darker corners of the hall, groaning, moaning, and humping was taking place. The men had been at war for a long time and were just as eager to spend themselves inside a tight pussy as Milo and Ragnar had been. A new generation would be born from the evening's celebrations, of that Milo was certain.

It had been agreed that Elizabeth would not be allowed out of their sight in the short term as she was more than clever enough to try some kind of escape attempt. Losing her to the east or the west would be disastrous, especially if she stirred an army up along the way. Her father was still beloved, and the memory of her mother who had died giving birth to her was strong in the minds of the peasants. Elizabeth needed to be kept under very strict control.

Milo took her to her bedchamber, posted two of his best men outside the door, and only then did he feel able to remove all his clothing and slide into bed beside Elizabeth. She was already fast asleep, exhausted by the events of the day. He watched her sleep for a little while, his chest feeling as though it might burst with pride. He had his prize, his princess.

• • • • • • •

The next thing Milo was aware of was waking up to the morning light with Elizabeth lying atop him, her slim fingers playing over the muscles of his chest. There was a look in her eye that Milo did not quite trust. His instinct was proved correct when she opened her mouth.

"You know he's going to kill you."

"Is that so?" Milo responded to the comment without fear. His cock was stiffening between his thighs again. He slid it casually between her pussy lips, sinking himself deep inside her naughty little cunt. If he was going to listen to her plot against the alliance, he may as well sate himself.

She let out a little gasp as she was penetrated yet again, almost distracted enough to stop talking as he held her buttocks and rocked his hips up and down to sluice his cock in and out of her tight, wet slit.

It felt so good to fuck her, even though she was a mischievous little wench who was certainly going to be a great deal of trouble. It was as if the silken glove of her sex was made just for him. The slow pace of his lovemaking meant that she was able to keep talking, albeit with a few gasps and moans along the way.

"It is common knowledge that there can only be one

king," Elizabeth said, her lips curling in a defiant smile even as his cock bottomed out deep inside her. "You have guards, but you will soon grow tired of sleeping with one eye open lest the barbarian's axe cleaves your skull."

"Hardly," Milo drawled, picking up the pace so she bucked against him with every stroke of his hips. "If either one of us were to betray the other, there would be an army waiting to avenge his death. Our men are loyal enough to mount a resistance. And if that were to happen, the east and west kingdoms would assuredly take advantage of that moment of weakness and stage their own invasions."

He trailed his fingers gently through her hair and took hold of a thick bunch of it as his cum roiled in his balls. Ordinarily, he would have made sure the sex was as pleasurable for her as it was for him, but she was misbehaving and she did not deserve to find climax, so he kept one hand in her hair and put the other on her hip, locking her nubile form atop him as he began hammering toward his climax.

Elizabeth stopped talking then and let out a long and continuous moan as he made hard, fast work of her tender pussy, ravaging her soft, wet lips with hard and ever faster strokes of his cock until he hauled her hard down against his body and locked her in place as a second dose of his seed soaked her vulnerable womb.

He did not let her go as he finished his thought, his lips moving against hers as he explained her mistake to her. "You see, Elizabeth, our pact is built on the strongest bond two men can share: a healthy respect for the ability of each to destroy the other."

Her green eyes narrowed as she realized her arguments were not having the desired effect upon him. Her seduction and reasoning were failing and she did not like it one little bit. "You assume the barbarian is intelligent enough to realize these things or care about them. You assume his love for brutality will not win out over his limited mental powers."

"And you assume that he is not standing directly behind you," Milo chuckled, easing Elizabeth up and off his cock. He rather enjoyed the way her face went pale moments before she was swept up into Ragnar's arms and turned over his lap. Ragnar had been standing in the doorway for quite some time, listening to Elizabeth do her very best to rid herself of him.

"This is for trying to plot against me, princess," Ragnar growled as his heavy palm began to beat what was starting to become a familiar tattoo against her bare bottom. "What a little traitor."

"I would have to have pledged my loyalty to you to be a traitor, idiot!"

Milo let out a low whistle. Elizabeth would surely regret that insult. Ragnar paused for a moment, both thick brows raised at the bold and rebellious princess. Of course her insolence would be punished, but Milo rather admired her spirit, as did Ragnar. His hand hovered in the air for a moment before clapping down against her round bottom in a hard slap that bought a pink print of his hand flashing across her skin.

"What will gain your loyalty, princess? How many times need I fill your tight little cunt before you realize who you belong to?"

"That which is owned will never be loyal, Ragnar," she managed to get the words out between gasps and yelps. It was quite a sight to see, the redheaded scrap of a young woman trying to resist the much larger barbarian.

He slid his hand between her legs and Milo knew he was rubbing her golden furred chalice. The expression in her eyes changed immediately, from flashing fire to reluctant desire. Ragnar wasn't going to argue with her. He was going to show her why she was wrong.

His muscular arm began to flex as his fingers slid inside her pussy. She was wet already, a combination of her own arousal and Milo's cum, which was still leaking out of her.

"You made a mess of her," Ragnar chuckled as Elizabeth

clutched at his leg, her back curving into a graceful arch as she raised her hips. She was very responsive to touch and Milo could not help but notice that both of their touches seemed to affect her in different ways.

With him, her passion flowed without reserve. His seduction left her without the wits to resist him. Ragnar, she fought, but enjoyed every bit of the struggle. Her eyes were bright and there was a half grin on her face between moans as she tried to free herself from his grasp and found her naughty pussy impaled on his thick fingers again and again. There could be no doubt that she was enjoying her rebellion, and that Ragnar was enjoying it too. A less spirited girl would have soon bored him, Milo was sure of that. But Elizabeth's fire kept Ragnar on his toes.

He let her go before she was entirely chastised and before she could climax, a decision Milo was sure was deliberate. She came tumbling off Ragnar's lap, rubbing her bottom and pouting furiously.

"On your knees," Ragnar commanded.

They both watched the struggle on her face. She was not inclined to be obedient and yet she knew very well that Ragnar would not tolerate disobedience. She slumped to her knees in a petulant fashion, arms folded across her chest as she looked at him with narrowed eyes.

"You're a brute," she complained.

Milo decided at that moment that it would be better to leave Elizabeth to her fate with the barbarian. His presence was complicating matters, and now that his cum was safely deposited in that tight pussy between her thighs, there was other business to attend to. He got up and began to dress while Elizabeth knelt there, pouting for all she was worth as his cum slowly slid out of her. As he left the room, Milo bent down and dropped a kiss on the top of her head.

"Be good," he said. "For your own sake."

• • • • • • •

Elizabeth should have listened. She did not listen. She was still very much aroused, and though King Lionheart's seed was swimming inside her, she wanted more. Needed more. Ragnar's barbaric insistence on treating her like a slave girl only served to inflame her rebellion and her desire.

"He's plotting against you," she told Ragnar. It was the same failed gambit that had not worked on Milo, but the barbarian was not as intellectually agile as Milo, she was sure of it. "He told me he intends to poison you. Be careful of the wine you drink and the meat you eat."

Ragnar let out a deep sigh and hung his head. Elizabeth had to hide a smile of glee. It was working!

The barbarian looked around the room. She didn't know what he was looking for until he picked up a satin scarf. It was pink and very fine, one of her favorite accessories. She was not sure what his plan was with it, especially when he began to twirl it so it curled up around on itself in a long twist. He took both ends of the scarf between his hands and approached her.

"Wha…"

The moment her mouth opened, Ragnar took a length of the twisted satin and pushed it between her lips. Elizabeth was confused until he tied it at the back of her head, gagging her. She no longer had the use of her tongue, so it was her eyes that asked the question that would have been on her lips.

"Your words are poison, princess. This will make you think about using them more carefully," Ragnar growled down at her.

She made a muffled response, glad he could not understand what she was saying.

"I cannot use your mouth, so I will have to take my pleasure with a different part of you," he observed almost casually.

He leaned down and picked her up from the floor as if she weighed nothing at all. It was quite something to feel the power of his body against hers, moving her around so easily. In all her days, Elizabeth had not suspected the true strength of a man like Ragnar.

Ragnar carried her across the room and pressed her body over the arm of a stuffed chair, leaving her bottom raised high. Stuck in that position, she waited to see what his will would be. She did not have to wait very long.

"Mmngggh!" She let out a little moan as he pushed his fingers inside her creamy cunt and swirled them about.

"I could take you here again," Ragnar mused. "But you seem rather full here, and there's another spot that is still untended."

Elizabeth did not know what he meant until his fingers withdrew from her pussy and traveled less than an inch upward before pressing against her bottom. She jerked in place and let out a squeal as Ragnar chuckled darkly and began to play with her anus, first with her own juices, which he rubbed all over the little winking bud, then with a small pitcher of oil that he commanded a maid to bring to him. Elizabeth saw the young woman's wide eyes as she made the delivery and she blushed furiously, knowing what she must look like with her legs splayed, her pussy coated in cum, her bottom hole beginning to give way to Ragnar's ministrations.

Her cheeks were spread and she felt trickles of thick oil running between them, over her anus and mound. It felt quite nice in both places, though she trembled at the idea of what he might do next. Without speaking, Ragnar pressed his finger inside the tight little aperture of her anus, making her stretch in the most embarrassing way. She had never conceived that a man would want to touch her there, let alone slide into the depths of her bottom. Her whole life, she had been warned that her vaginal virginity was the most important virtue she had, but now she was learning there was another kind of much more sensitive virginity to lose—and Ragnar was about to take it.

If she had been able to speak, she would have called him a filthy brute, an absolute savage. But all she could do was moan into the gag as he worked first one, then two fingers slowly in and out of her bottom hole.

When there was no longer as much resistance to the passage of his fingers as there had been in the beginning, Ragnar withdrew his fingers and pressed his thick, hard cock to her bottom hole. Elizabeth wriggled furiously in an attempt to avoid it, but all that did was help him as his thick oily cock speared slowly inside the ring of muscle. Throughout the anal preparations her pussy had been yearning for his hard rod, but it went totally untended as Ragnar began to take her bottom in slow, short but powerful strokes, working himself deeper inside her tightest, hottest hole with every motion. It was far from comfortable, but Elizabeth had little choice but to endure this punitive seduction.

Moaning against the gag, she was as helpless as she had ever been. His hands kept her cheeks spread wide as he plundered her in the most embarrassing way possible. She was most chastised by this treatment, which aroused her as much as it shamed her. Both sets of cheeks blushed profusely as her anal muscles began to relax and allow him easier passage, his thick rod making an easy entry over and over again. Ragnar did not lecture during his punishments. His actions did all the speaking for him, his hands keeping her locked in place so that she could barely squirm.

The pace increased until he was fucking her bottom much as he would her pussy, his cock slamming deep into her without mercy or respite. Far from being painful, it was driving her arousal to greater heights. Her juices were sluicing down her thighs, coating her inner legs with a sheen of need that went untended as Ragnar satisfied himself with her ass.

His primal grunting and the swelling of his cock made her let out a little wail. He was going to come in her bottom. She could barely believe it, and yet she knew what the furious pounding of his hips meant as he pushed her forward, her clit finally getting some attention if only because it was grinding against the fabric of the chair as he pinned her in place and fucked her for all she was worth.

She was so very well filled, so totally taken by his desire that she found herself swept up in the orgasmic wave along with him, coming as hard as he when he thrust himself as deep as he could go and let his seed flood her bottom in great welling spurts.

Grunting with pleasure, Ragnar pulled the gag from her mouth and kissed her deeply with a passion that drove all thoughts of rebellion or shame or fear from her mind. Elizabeth very much wanted to be outraged, but wrapped in his arms and pressed against the hard lines of his body, she felt comfort and security. Two words she would never have associated with Ragnar in a hundred years.

# CHAPTER FOUR

After a long day in the company and custody of the barbarian, Elizabeth took the chance to slip out of his bed that evening and clear her head by walking the halls of the palace. So much had changed and yet so much was still the same. She was still in her ancestral home. The floors still felt the same beneath her feet. It was quite disorienting to try to fathom the way her world was changing, both externally and internally. She was not the same woman she had been days ago. She was a new creature, one who had taken two men inside her body in different and sometimes shameful ways.

As she walked and thought, she noticed that there was a light flickering in the library. She followed it out of curiosity, moving softly in her bare feet so as to avoid detection. She tiptoed between the stacks of scrolls and books to find King Lionheart sitting alone.

He was wearing a simple shirt, the front of it open halfway down his chest. The light from the candle was flickering against the gold hue of his hair and the side of his face in a way that made her heart flutter much like that flame.

"Hello, princess," Milo drawled. He must have heard her coming, or breathing; she did not know how he had detected her presence. He hadn't moved an inch since she entered the room. The way he said the word 'princess' seemed to be more an endearment than a title in his cultured voice.

"Hello," she said, suddenly feeling rather shy. In the quiet of the room and the light of the single candle, she felt less like his captive and more like a shy new bride.

Milo closed the manuscript he had been reading and extending his hand to her as she stepped around to look at him. She put her small, slim hand into his and allowed him to draw her down into a sitting position on his lap. She could not help an involuntary wince as she settled her round cheeks against his hard thighs.

"A sore behind, hmm?" There was some sympathy in his voice, a softness she had not heard before.

She did not answer his question at first. Her behavior was answer enough. There was not just the pain of her punished cheeks to contend with, there was also the ache deeper inside her bottom where the muscle had been stretched by the repeated passage of Ragnar's cock.

"Very," she said softly.

Milo made another sympathetic sound and ran his hand through her hair in a gentle caress. "Taunting the barbarian was not all you wanted it to be, then... or perhaps it was?"

She blushed and gave a little giggle as he pressed his mouth to her neck in a kiss. "You would be a handful for any man, but I think between us we have some chance of taming you, princess."

"I was never wild," she replied with a little smile.

"Says the young lady who brandished a dagger the first night we met. You were hardly a willing captive, Elizabeth." His hand was tracing along the outside of her thigh in a slow caress as his lips moved along her neck to her collarbone.

She felt a delightful shiver rushing through her flesh as Milo slowly explored her body's less obvious erogenous zones, finding places she hadn't known felt good. His mouth traveled back up her neck and to a spot just below her ear.

"Were you naughty for Ragnar, princess?"

"No?" Her voice sounded high and innocent even though it was certainly a lie.

"Mhm. I think you were," Milo said. "You have not rested for a moment since we claimed you, trying to unsettle an unsteady alliance. I give you credit, princess, you have admirable political instincts."

She would likely have engaged in the conversation a great deal more if his hand had not slid over her thigh and settled between her legs, the blade of his fingers pressing the silk of her robe against the slit of her womanhood.

"I'm not being naughty with you," she moaned softly.

"Oh, but you are." He started slowly massaging her still soaking pussy. "You came upon me with such stealthy footsteps. You wished to observe me without being observed. Didn't you."

She could barely think, let alone reply as her legs spread to allow him greater access to her silk-clad mound. Milo slowly worked his fingers up and down her lips, the flat of three of his nails lightly scratching against her yearning pussy.

"Hmm, princess?" he prompted her gently.

"I wasn't spying," she moaned. "I didn't know who was in here."

"And what were you doing creeping about the castle in the middle of the night?"

"Ragnar was asleep," she said. "And I wasn't tired."

"Weren't tired," he said. "Well, maybe you need to be tired out so you can sleep as you should be sleeping."

"You should be sleeping too," she replied. "It is just as late for you as it is for me."

"A king may stay up as late as he likes," Milo chuckled, apparently enjoying their gentle banter. "But let us go to bed together and see if we cannot bring one another to sleep."

He stood up, supporting Elizabeth against his chest with his arm under her bottom while he picked up the candle with the other. She was surprised at his easy strength as he rose. Compared to Ragnar's burlier frame, Milo could appear slight, but he was nothing of the kind. She let her head rest against his shoulder as he carried her to the chamber he had taken for himself. Once upon a time it had been her mother's. Many of the original furnishings remained, including her mother's crest embroidered on a flag that hung on the north wall. She was glad to see that it had not been damaged or moved.

The bed was positioned in such a way that two beams of light intersected on the sheets. Normally the shutters would have been closed against the light, but on that evening they were wide open and sweet fresh air filled the room, along with the moon's silver glow.

Milo blew the candle out and put it down. There was no need for it anymore; indeed, the room seemed brighter without its intrusive flame. He carried Elizabeth all the way to the bed and let her slide down upon the coverlet.

"Are you tired yet, princess?" He asked the question gently as he stood next to the bed, looking down at her with a smiling gaze. He could seem almost soft at times, and yet Elizabeth knew all too well that there was nothing soft in his desire or his intent either. He was playing with her, teasing her with the prospect of not having her carnal desires satisfied. She had a burning between her thighs from where he had caressed her, a sensation she knew would not abate until he slid his cock deep inside her.

"I am most awake," she said, reclining into an elegant position that left the curve of her breast exposed under the robe. Seduction was a game that could easily be played by two people. She saw the narrowing of his eyes as she arched her back and let the hardening nub of her nipple slide back and forth below the satin of her gown.

He was hungry and he was lean, like a rogue wolf looking for tender prey. He slid onto the bed between her legs, spreading them so he could look between her thighs. His brow rose slowly as he took in the untouched state of her pouting lower lips.

"I can smell him on you," he said, rubbing his hand over her mound, the red curling fur slick with her juices as he cupped her pussy. "But he didn't take you here, did he?" Milo asked the question in his erotic drawl. "Where did he take you, princess?"

She couldn't bring herself to say the words at first. She felt a sudden heat rush across her face as she blushed profusely.

Milo slid down next to her on the bed, his hand roaming from her mound, over her hip, to her sore cheeks. "Tell me where he took you, Elizabeth."

She felt his fingers slide against her lower lips, part them and find the bud of her clit. Her hips jolted as his fingers closed over it, pinching lightly.

"Tell me, princess," he urged, drawing the confession out of her with a tightening of his fingers.

"In... my bottom," she finally admitted in a soft moan.

"Ah." Milo's hand slid over her rear cheeks in a slow caress. "He fucked your tight little bottom. And how did that feel? Did it hurt, or..." He leaned in, his lips next to her ear. "Did you like it?"

She was squirming furiously now, her hips gyrating as she shook her head. "Of course not."

"I'm not sure I believe you, princess." His hand clamped on her hip and made her still her movements.

Ragnar had fucked her bottom, but it was Milo who was making her feel the force of it to the very core. He intensified everything, leaving no feeling or experience to lie unexamined. Elizabeth let out a little whimper, hoping to avoid the question, hoping more to avoid the knowing in his eyes.

"He took you there and it felt good, didn't it, Elizabeth?" He used her name in that gentle, refined drawl and she felt her inner walls clench with desire.

"You can admit it, my sweet princess... you were made to be taken by kings. There is no shame in it."

He pushed his hips forward and let the hard ridge of his cock press against her belly, then turned her on her side. Whether he said there was shame in it or not, she could not stop her blushing, not even as he began to push his cock inside her slick pussy and thrust slowly.

As she felt him fill her, Elizabeth let out a sigh of pure contentment and desire. From the moment Ragnar had laid hands on her, she had been burning to feel the hard flesh of a man inside her tight walls. It had been a long time spent in suspended arousal and every part of her body thrilled to Milo's cock.

He was unhurried, rolling on his back to pull her atop him and slowly guide her hips up and down, gliding her wet pussy along his cock. She rose up and looked down at him, taking in the masculine lines of his body and face. Some force far greater than them all had formed him to be a king, that much was obvious to her. He was the embodiment of regal authority, his face a mask of lust as he angled his hips up to make his cock slide as deep as possible inside her tightening walls.

"He was a fool," Milo said. "No sons will be born from spending himself in your bottom. It's your cunt that must be filled."

Elizabeth felt the inner tremors starting all over again at his words. It was one thing to be fucked. It was another thing to be... well... bred. This was no casual sex act. This was a man who had filled her sensitive pussy twice already and was about to do it for a third time. Why did her body find the prospect so delicious? Why did she feel hot and cold and tingly? Why were her toes curling and her inner walls clenching? She did not know, she could not know, all she could do was succumb to the climax she had been denied that morning.

"Yes, princess!" Milo praised her and urged her on as she arched against him, her cunt clenching desperately as a wail of pure release escaped her throat and she came on his cock, her juices mixing with the thrusting spurts of his seed as Milo came along with her, his orgasm triggered by hers as he held her locked on his cock, his cum pushed deep inside her over and over again with slow, deliberate thrusts of his slowly softening rod.

In the aftermath of her breeding, for that was what she now knew it to be, Elizabeth laid in the bed next to Milo, his arm wrapped around her waist to keep her securely locked against his body. She could feel his cum slowly seeping out of her and knew that there was more inside. He had flooded her with potent semen and though perhaps it would not take that day, one day it would.

Milo slept beside her, but Elizabeth's eyes stayed open long into the night.

# CHAPTER FIVE

The next morning, Elizabeth sat in the window of her tower room and watched the soldiers below be drilled by the kings in quite a different fashion to the way she had been drilled by the same.

Milo and Ragnar were blending their military styles and creating a greater force between them than either had commanded on their own. The generals from each of their armies were working with the units of the other's soldiers. It was the very early days, but it was quite apparent that they had more than maintaining their borders in mind. Elizabeth had the feeling she was watching the beginnings of something more than an alliance... she was looking at the infancy of an empire.

The thought left her with mixed feelings. For a hundred years, the five kingdoms had been stable. Now, in a matter of a few months there were just three kingdoms—and it was all her fault. Milo and Ragnar had come for her and the world was no longer the same.

"If my father had seen this..." Elizabeth shook her head. "Had I been born a male, this would not be happening."

Her maid shot her a worried look. "Women cannot be

men, princess."

"No, but if I were to have been born one…" Elizabeth blinked back tears that rose from frustration. Her father's kingdom was gone, replaced with an abominable alliance between a barbarian and a wicked king. She was but a princess, limited in her ability to resist their designs and desires.

"You will bear the next one," her maid said in a way that Elizabeth was sure was supposed to be comforting.

She laid her head on her hands and looked down at the two men whose seed was even now vying to be the first to take hold in her belly. Was that truly the limit of her power? To hope that she could bring forth some male heir who might right what was now going wrong? By the time such an heir were grown, this would be ancient history.

Sooner or later, she would bear an heir to one of them. That much she did know. Their lovemaking was ardent and frequent. They bathed her womb in their seed regularly, and she knew what the outcome of that would inevitably be. One of the men below would soon win the war for her womb… but which one?

Milo was very handsome, but he was equally wicked, she was absolutely sure of that. His ambition was the most frightening thing about him. She had seen it blaze in his eyes many times, often while he was looking at her. His desire for her was tied to political fortunes, she was sure of that. He seemed to hold some knowledge that Ragnar did not, some secret that twinkled in his eye. He had often ensconced himself in her father's libraries. He seemed to have a particular purpose among the manuscripts, but whatever that purpose was, he kept it to himself.

Ragnar's lust was more simple to untangle. He wanted a royal bride and she was one. He was happy to conquer her and her resistance excited him. She would spend a lifetime being conquered by him, until some man or beast conquered him in turn. He was not a man who could or would lead a quiet life, she was almost certain of that.

She could not pick a favorite among them, nor could she name one worse than the other. They were so dissimilar as to avoid all meaningful comparison. Her head swam and her stomach performed flips inside her belly as she tried to think her way out of the unthinkable conundrum she found herself in.

"I must be free of this," she declared. "If only for an hour or two."

With that declaration, she made her way down to the courtyard, making for the kings with her head held high. It was not her wont to interfere in training usually, but she could no longer abide her confinement.

The soldiers and barbarians parted as she walked through the crowd, and Milo and Ragnar smiled as she made her way across to them. They seemed pleased to see her, a fact that warmed her heart but caused more confusion in her mind. She wanted to hate them for what they were doing to Ammerdale, and to her, but when she looked into their faces, she felt an emotion completely other than hate.

"What can we do for you, princess?" There was a kind indulgence in Milo's tone, which Elizabeth found encouraging.

"I wish to go to the market," she said. "I am bored."

Milo and Ragnar looked at one another, then nodded. "Very well," Milo said. "You may go to the market, but you will do so under guard."

She sighed. They did not understand. It was not the market she wanted to see. She wanted some freedom from the constant confinement. She wanted to clear her mind and feel herself a person among people, not a princess locked in a role that forever chained her.

"You think anyone will dare touch me, knowing that I am the possession of two kings? You think I am not safe in my own market? You think someone would risk your ire to harm me? Someone with so little respect for you that they would so much as touch a hair on my head?"

Her argument won Ragnar first, as she knew it would.

The barbarian did not like any insinuation that he might not be universally feared. King Lionheart was a more difficult sell. Milo cocked his head to the side and gave her a piercing look.

"Do you have some idea of escape, Elizabeth?"

"No," she said, all the more convincing for telling the truth. "I have not been permitted outside the castle walls in months. Being able to walk in the market is escape enough for me."

Her tone must have been sincere enough to tug at his heartstrings. Or perhaps it was the way she made her eyes wide and batted her lashes. Whatever it was, he agreed.

"Our men are guarding the markets, that much is true," he said. "You should be safe enough. Very well. Go and enjoy yourself. Be sure to be back in time for dinner. If we do not see you by the gathering of dusk, we will send men after you, and if we have to do that, you will be punished."

Elizabeth tried not to glower at him. She did not at all appreciate being threatened with discipline. Her father had never disciplined her, but Milo seemed to think she needed it almost constantly. She forced a smile on her face and bent into a little curtsey.

"Thank you," she said, trying not to grit the words out between her teeth. "I will see you soon."

The castle gates were a short walk away. She made toward them without looking back over her shoulder. She didn't need to in order to know that both Milo's and Ragnar's eyes were on her. She could feel them watching her as she stepped boldly out into the unknown... well, not quite the unknown, but the greater castle grounds, really. Ammerdale City was constructed in a series of concentric circles, through which both Milo's and Ragnar's forces had penetrated roughly.

The market was more or less directly outside the castle gates, valuable wares and produce kept relatively safe. It was a mixture of stalls and small buildings and tents and even simple carts containing fruits and vegetables. Elizabeth smiled a little as the chatter of commerce began to envelop her. It had been a very long time since she had been permitted to go out in such a fashion. She had followed her father's orders and stayed in the castle even after his death. If Ragnar and Milo had not been successful in their conquest, she would likely still be up in the tower. But she had very much missed the market, not only because of the exotic goods that occasionally made their way to Ammerdale, but because of the people who spoke loudly and excitedly, each salesman and woman crying their wares to the crowds. Despite the war, it had remained a bustling commercial hub, and because the kings had been eager to keep the trade flowing, the market was much as Elizabeth remembered it.

As Elizabeth walked through the stalls, she became faintly aware that there were two hulking guards lurking in the mid-distance, obviously sent to follow her. She tried to dodge into the thickest groups of people to avoid the men tailing her, but they were very persistent. She cursed King Lionheart's name. Milo had granted her a measure of freedom, but he was also intent on making sure she was on a leash of some sort no matter where she went or what she did. It was Milo behind the spies, she was sure of that.

For several minutes, Elizabeth more or less stomped around the market. Some of the traders tried to engage her with their wares, but she was not interested. She wanted to breathe, to be alone in the crowd. But it seemed impossible until someone reached out, took hold of her arm, and drew her into a little alley between stalls that she herself had not noticed.

Elizabeth was quite frightened until she saw that the person holding her was a wizened old woman lurking in a very small stall, more a fabric-draped booth, really.

"Elizabeth," the old lady said, pushing back the hood of her dress to reveal a gnarled, wizened face. "You are the princess of prophecy. The one whose womb will bear a king who will unite all nations."

Elizabeth looked down at her stomach. It did not look or feel any different than it ever had, and though she knew her womb was tucked away somewhere in the general region, she didn't feel powerful. She had spent every moment since the invasion and conquest feeling rather small and helpless.

"Do not despair." The old woman's voice softened. She reached out and tucked a strand of Elizabeth's red hair behind her ear in an affectionate gesture, which made Elizabeth smile a little. The smallest kindness truly was welcome in these confusing and trying times. "The future holds more wealth and prosperity than you can imagine."

Wealth and prosperity were not at the forefront of Elizabeth's mind, but she smiled and acknowledged the words. The woman was trying to comfort her, and she very much appreciated the effort. Certainly King Milo and King Ragnar had been of little comfort in their various ways.

"I have seen the future, princess," the woman said. "And I will tell you, if you will cross my palm with silver."

Elizabeth had been attended by many fortune tellers in the past. Sometimes they were correct, other times they were wildly incorrect, but they were always rather interesting. She needed the distraction, so she produced more than silver. She pressed three gold pieces into the old woman's palm.

"Thank you, princess." The woman smiled, clenched her palm, and then the gold was gone. It was a trick Elizabeth had seen before, but it was no less impressive for the repetition.

Elizabeth waited to hear what her prosperous future would be, but instead of speaking, the old woman took a small vial from her robes and gave it to Elizabeth.

"Drink this," she said. "And you will see all you need to see, you will see the truth of all things laid out before you in a grand cascade."

Elizabeth looked at it dubiously. "What is in it?"

"Liquid truth," the old woman said with a smile. "But

the truth is not for everybody, and cannot be heard with the ears. It must be seen with the mind. If you wish to see, take the medicine."

Elizabeth was a sensible young woman in many respects who certainly did not go about drinking strange substances given to her by elderly strangers, but in her stressed, emotional, tired state, she found herself not just making sure the vial was secreted in her dress, but rather enjoying the feel of it. It was a little capsule of freedom, or at least, it felt that way to her.

"Thank you," she said. "Do you have any other advice for me?"

"The true character of men is revealed in time," the old woman said. "Nothing can be known in bed until it has been known in the world beyond the bedroom."

"So, I shouldn't give my heart to men who are good in bed?"

"I did not say that," the old woman cackled. "You will know more when you have taken your medicine."

Elizabeth thanked the woman and moved back out into the crowded market. She felt as though she had some clarity and advantage now, though she did not know why. Meeting the woman had given her a sense of independence; she now had a little secret all of her own hidden in her skirts. Nobody knew it, certainly not the spies who she spotted searching the crowd to little avail.

She spent a little time dodging the spies, but ultimately returned to the castle well within her curfew. Milo and Ragnar seemed surprised to see her at the appointed dinner hour. They had likely expected her to disobey them, and they were right to. She had certainly planned on doing so before the old lady gave her a way to keep her rebellion more secret.

They ate dinner together, all three of them alone at a small round table. Milo sat to Elizabeth's right, Ragnar to her left. The conversation mostly took place between the men at first; they were excited about the development of their armies, and allocating resources from what had been Elizabeth's kingdom further afield.

She held her tongue, knowing it was better to gather information in silence than argue with either of her royal lovers. Eventually, however, the conversation turned to her exploits, as pedestrian as they had been.

"Did you enjoy your time in the markets, princess?" Milo asked the question.

"There were a great many more traders," Elizabeth said. "All manner of interesting diversions." She returned to her meal quickly, hoping they would not notice her reluctance to speak. Her opinion and thoughts had not been solicited by either man before, so she doubted they would take note of it.

"You returned well within your curfew," Milo noted.

"I would not dare risk punishment," Elizabeth replied sweetly. "After you were so kind to give me leave to visit the market."

"She is up to something," Ragnar drawled.

"Yes," Milo agreed. "I think she is."

Elizabeth gave a little shrug and hoped she looked suitably unbothered, though her heart was beginning to pound and her palms were starting to sweat. How did they know? Had the soldiers seen something? Said something? Surely not. Nobody had seen what was happening in the little stall. The curtain had obscured it all.

"What did you buy?" Ragnar asked the question.

"Nothing," Elizabeth lied.

"Do you know any woman who, given ample gold and a day free in the markets, purchases nothing?" Milo addressed the question to Ragnar, not her.

"I do not," Ragnar said. His dark eyes had not left her face, and she realized that his expression was not playfully inquisitive as Milo's was. It was outright suspicious and more than a little concerning. "I have also never known a young woman not to get into trouble when left to her own devices."

"You may have known women, but you have never known *me* before," Elizabeth replied rather pertly. "And I am offended by each of your accusations. I followed the rules as you set them out, and in return I am interrogated like some prisoner. It would be easier if you were to keep me in the dungeons and forego any appearance of kindness."

She gave both of them an annoyed glare, hoping it would stop the line of questioning.

"Being prickly won't change anything, princess," Milo said. "What did you do at the market?"

"Didn't your spies tell you?"

He didn't look ashamed in the slightest as she accused him of spying on her. He also didn't deny it.

"My men lost track of you somehow."

"Not terribly good spies then, are they?"

Milo cut his eyes at her. "I want to know where you went and what you did. It's obvious that you were up to no good."

Up to no good? Why would he assume such a thing? Elizabeth narrowed her eyes at him and made no further response. She would not dignify his probing with an answer. She certainly did not owe him one. She put a little meat on her fork and then put the fork to her mouth and chewed the morsel in one of the most deafening silences she had experienced in memory.

"Princess," Milo drawled in that deceptively casual tone he used on occasion. "I am sure Ragnar and I can extract an answer from you if you refuse…"

Very well. He wished to hear a story? She would tell him one. Elizabeth put her fork down, folded her hands in front of her and began to speak as if reciting from some unwritten book of boring lies.

"First I went to a fruit stall. There were apples, red and green and some partway between. I thought about purchasing one, but I was not hungry at the time and carrying an apple about seemed impractical. Then I visited a little shop where a woman with one foot was selling carvings for good luck. There was a toad I rather liked… it looked like you, Ragnar."

Ragnar let out a gruff guffaw as he stood, reached for her and caught her in his grasp before she could make a dash to safety.

"You insolent little minx," he growled down at her. Seated, he had not seemed nearly as imposing as he now did, holding her in his powerful hands. The man was built along the lines of a colossus. She felt a tremor pass through her body, but it wasn't fear. It was the excitement of rebellion. Meeting the old lady had reminded Elizabeth that she was not merely some helpless princess at the mercy of two tyrannical kings… she was a princess with options and choices. At least, that was what she was telling herself in that moment, even as Ragnar lifted her clear off her feet so her nose was pressed against his.

"Do you want a spanking, princess? Are you trying to get yourself into trouble? Or have you forgotten your manners and respect?"

"So many questions," Elizabeth replied. "I'm not sure you'd be able to follow the answers if I were to give them."

"The answer is obviously yes to all three," Ragnar growled, his expression growing most displeased. "You will respect me, princess. Or you will pay the price."

"You think you can spank me into respecting you? You think I respect either of you?" She threw a rebellious look over at Milo, who had become quite stone-faced during her exchange with Ragnar. "You have taken me captive, made me your prisoner. You have taken my body…"

"We have taken nothing you did not willingly give, princess," Ragnar reminded her. "You have begged for our cocks and our seed time and time again, and this time you will ask for your spanking before you receive it."

Elizabeth looked at him with utter incredulity. "I can assure you I will not."

Ragnar's hand tightened briefly, holding her in place as

his leg swept around behind hers, putting her neatly on her knees. His grasp on her arm meant that her descent was not as violent as it might have been, she simply found herself kneeling in front of the barbarian with little choice in the matter.

"You will stay there until you do," he growled.

She made to get up, in another show of defiance, but Ragnar pressed her back to her knees with little in the way of effort.

"Down, girl," he drawled, his dark eyes lighting with dominant pleasure. "Ask me nicely for a spanking, then you can get up—and go over my knee."

It wasn't fair. There was no way for her to escape from the uncomfortable position that was already beginning to make her knees feel rather sore, but to ask Ragnar to spank her. He stood in front of her, his long legs spread shoulder width apart, his big hands rubbing together in punitive anticipation.

He was not as stupid as he looked. He had neatly devised a situation in which not only would he inevitably punish her, but in the meantime she would punish herself. The longer she rebelled, the more uncomfortable she'd ultimately be.

She looked back to Milo for some kind of salvation, but he was sitting back with his arms folded across his chest, his body language speaking volumes. She was on her own for this one—and she was probably fortunate that he was not joining with Ragnar in this punishment.

There was one thing for it. Elizabeth looked up at Ragnar with wide eyes that became watery very quickly. "I'm sorry," she said softly, batting her lashes as a single tear began to trace down her cheek. "I've been under so very much strain. My nerves are stretched to their very limits. I think I may be experiencing a nervous hysteria of some kind. You should call for a physician."

Ragnar shook his head firmly, not buying her tearful words one little bit.

"A good thrashing is all you need to settle those nerves,"

he said. "Ask for what you need, and you will receive it, princess."

Of course the brute did not care for her feelings. He did not care for her at all. He was using her for his carnal desires and in the hopes of filling her womb. Nothing more and nothing less. Her tears dried almost instantly as she expressed her fury.

"You will regret this!" She hissed the words. "I may only be a princess, but I have more power at my disposal than you could ever imagine."

"Threats, Elizabeth? Very unwise."

Ragnar's use of her given name gave her pause for thought, as did the cold growl in which her name was uttered. He was not pleased with her, not in the slightest. This would end painfully, she was sure of that. All she could hope for was to inflict a little suffering in return. She could not physically match him, but she could bruise his ego.

"A threat you're afraid of, because you've come a very long way to be the pawn of another king. That's right," she said as Ragnar's eyes narrowed. "You came here to claim a kingdom, and a princess. But you have not claimed a single thing. You have been tricked by a much smarter, wiser man into not only giving up this kingdom... but your own as well. Milo has taken your men, your country, and your kingship."

"Elizabeth!" Milo's voice rang out sharply. "I have told you not to try these manipulative tactics to cause unrest. They did not work before and they will not work now."

"Of course you have," she shot back. "You don't want him to know what you're doing. You want him to be distracted by fucking me."

"That's not true..."

"I was there the night you made your pact," she interrupted. "Did you think about it, Ragnar? Milo thought about it. Your men stormed the castle, didn't they. His came after. You lost several good soldiers. He lost none. He used you and your warriors as a shield and he met you in my chamber, where he knew you would be distracted…" She was speaking swiftly now as the words and ideas fell into place. She didn't strictly know that what she was saying was true, but it sounded true enough, and she could see by Ragnar's eyes, which were now darting between her and Milo, that they were having an effect on the barbarian king.

There was a very long silence as Ragnar stared at Milo with something like murder in his eyes. Elizabeth held her breath, wondering if perhaps she had said too much—or not enough.

"I'm going to put the girl away," Ragnar finally said. "And we are going to talk."

Elizabeth did her best to hide her glee as Ragnar marched her to her chambers. Even once locked away, she was still rather pleased with herself. She had gotten under both her captors' skins, and she had risen from her knees without asking for a spanking. She had won. For the very first time, she had won.

She curled up on her bed, smiling quite broadly to herself. So this was what triumph felt like. She rather liked it.

# CHAPTER SIX

"That girl is not stupid," Ragnar said gruffly, seating himself on the chair before the fire. He looked at Milo with no small measure of concern. "Have I been played for a fool, pretty king? Have you been toying with me all this time?"

Milo's brow quirked at the 'pretty king' insult, but he kept his cool. Elizabeth had left more than a little turbulence in her wake. She had aggravated Ragnar and an annoyed barbarian was no joke. Milo could see the tension held in Ragnar's shoulders and arms. The man was bristling visibly, his muscles flexed in preparation for a fight Milo sincerely hoped would not happen.

"I made a pact with you in good faith, Ragnar. We came to the same place at the same time, wanting the same thing. The choice was to kill one another, or build an alliance. We chose the latter. The question is, do you trust me, or do you trust the minx who is doing everything in her power to cause trouble between us?" Milo chuckled darkly. "She makes a sport of it, Ragnar. Her words are more dangerous than poisoned arrows at times. She will bring us down if we are not careful—and perhaps, even if we are."

Ragnar let out a long sigh. "This princess is more trouble

than I had bargained for." He lifted his powerful head and looked Milo in the eye. "As are you. When I set out from my capital, I intended to bring back a bride. I have an errant girl and an unlikely ally—maybe an untrustworthy one."

"Fate rarely delivers what men intend for her to deliver," Milo smiled. "Our alliance will need to be strong to contend with the challenges across our borders—and in our bedrooms."

"So there is no truth in what she says? There can be no doubt you wield some command over my forces and my territory."

"And you mine," Milo replied. "The minx said what she said to you because she knew it would get under your skin, but she could have said precisely the same thing to me."

"She was right that my men pressed first and yours followed," Ragnar pressed on. "Had you been but an hour later, she would have been mine. Had you been an hour earlier, you would have met the palace guard. Your timing was suspicious, Milo. Do you not admit that?"

"My scouts did report that you were poised to breach the castle," Milo admitted. "We were not prepared. I took a small force and met you at the top. Yes, I profited by your actions, but I did not set out to take anything from you that I have not wanted just as long as you. I fought just as hard and just as long as you did."

"Not quite as long," Ragnar growled, rising to his feet. "And not quite as hard. The princess is right. You used me, and now you claim my lands as yours."

Milo stood his ground as the barbarian closed the distance between them. Ragnar was fraction taller and much broader and in that moment was deeply threatening. There was no doubt in Milo's mind that if he showed the slightest sliver of weakness, there would be a nasty altercation.

Ragnar had claimed his throne through battle. Milo had inherited his. They were very different men with very different skills and though Ragnar would not have believed him if he had said it in the moment, Milo admired him deeply.

"What are you going to do, Ragnar?" Milo asked the question calmly. "Try to kill me?"

"I should snap your neck." Ragnar snarled the words, his breath condensing in the air. In that moment, he looked like a mythical Minotaur, all strength and anger.

"No, you should stop letting a scrap of a female dictate your actions," Milo said, knowing his words might anger Ragnar more. "She's been trying to get us to fight from the beginning."

"You keep saying that." Ragnar closed the distance between them, his chest pressing against Milo's. There was no space between them now, just a sliver of light between their noses. Milo could smell the man and feel his breath, as well as his anger. In spite of his efforts to maintain self-control, his anger was starting to flare as well. It glowed bright at Ragnar's next words. "I think you're afraid to fight."

"I have nothing to fear from you," Milo replied, his voice cold like steel.

"You have everything to fear," Ragnar growled in return. He took another step, walking more or less through Milo, pushing him back with the bulk of his body. It was a challenge, one that could not be allowed to go unanswered.

Milo wasn't actually sure who swung first. One moment they were facing off, the next fists were flying. In spite of the skillful and powerful nature of their blows, nobody made contact in the initial flurry. They backed off and stared at one another with a mixture of smugness and surprise. Ragnar looked shaken, and Milo knew why. The barbarian had counted on being able to flatten him with a single punch. What the barbarian king did not know was that Milo had served as a squire since his teen years and drilled as hard as any of his father's soldiers. He knew very well how not to be hit. He also knew how to grapple. He pressed the advantage of the moment and took hold of Ragnar by the upper arms, drawing close so that the barbarian could not bring the brunt of his force to bear.

Ragnar's size was a disadvantage in the close grip of battle, where their hard bodies pressed together, Milo's leg sliding between the barbarian's hairy thighs to hook around his lower leg and send him tumbling to the floor head over heels.

He grabbed Milo on his way down, bringing the younger man with him. Sweat was already dripping down both their bodies as they grappled for control. Milo could see surprise in Ragnar's eyes as he realized that Milo was an even match for him. From the moment of their meeting, there had been an animal tension in Ragnar's assumption that he was the physically dominant one. But he had not counted on conditioning or technique and now it was Milo's arm pressed against his throat even as he wrapped his hands about Milo's neck.

"Look at what she has reduced us to," Milo growled. "Rolling around on the ground and snapping at one another like dogs. Is it really me you want to be pressed against, Ragnar?"

"You're an impudent pup," the barbarian growled.

"You're an old dog distracted by the scent of a little bitch," Milo snapped back. His hair was falling into his eyes as he locked his legs around Ragnar in an attempt to put the barbarian into a submission hold while avoiding Ragnar's own efforts to crush his windpipe.

They were much more evenly matched than either of them had suspected. Milo could see the surprise in Ragnar's eyes growing with every passing moment. It was no longer a matter of strength, it was a matter of stamina. They were locked together, each waiting for the other to tire.

As seconds turned to minutes, the clinch started to become somewhat silly. The rage that had first impelled them to fight had faded and now they found themselves locked in an uncomfortable embrace.

"Do you still want me as an enemy, Ragnar?" Milo asked the question between clenched teeth. The barbarian's hands were still at his neck, making breathing somewhat challenging. His own elbow pressed against Ragnar's windpipe prevented the warrior from making a more aggressive attempt to cut his life short.

"Enemy? You are not an enemy," Ragnar replied. "You're a pup."

"This pup is about to take your last breath," Milo growled back, putting more pressure on the barbarian's windpipe. "What does that make you? A kitten?"

"A kitten?" Ragnar burst out with sudden laughter. "All my life, I have never been called a kitten." His grip loosened with his mirth, and soon they broke apart, both grinning broadly in the way only men who have tested one another's mettle and found the other able can.

"You will have to teach my men those holds you used," Ragnar said, rubbing his neck. "They make a mockery of a man's strength."

Milo straightened his shirt and flashed a broad smile. "There is more to life than brute force—as Elizabeth well knows. The little minx had her way with us just now. She slipped her guards, got up to God knows what in the markets, spoke churlishly to us, and set us at one another's throats."

"What can we do to stop her?" Ragnar shrugged the question.

"We must tame her, thoroughly," Milo announced. "We must remove the very last shreds of resistance from her and teach her that her place is at our feet. She must accept this willingly, to the core of her being. There must be joy in her submission. It is not enough for us to punish and dominate; we must seduce her into becoming what we both well know she could be."

"So, she gets the thrashing she deserves?" Ragnar's grin became lustful.

"Oh, she absolutely does—and more besides."

# CHAPTER SEVEN

The moment the door to her chamber opened to reveal two masculine figures standing side by side, Elizabeth knew she was in trouble. There was something stern and staunch about their demeanor, something that suggested an intent she would not enjoy.

Milo's handsome face, which usually carried at least a hint of good humor, was entirely devoid of any merriment. And Ragnar, he looked as fierce as any barbarian could. Twin trickles of fear and arousal raced through her body as she sat up in bed, wrapped her arms about her knees, and watched them come closer with no small measure of trepidation.

"Remove your dress, princess," Milo ordered. "You will be punished nude."

"Punished? For what?"

"Attempting to manipulate us."

"Attempting?" She let the question hang in the air. There was little point playing innocent now. She had not been subtle and clearly they had worked out their differences before coming to her. Now there were two very large, very capable, very determined men, one of whom was holding a thick leather belt, the other who picked up one of her satin slippers on his way in.

"I don't think that will fit you, Ragnar," she said with a smile that was a little too bright. "But I'd like to see you try to put it on. Pink is your color."

"Red is yours, princess," Ragnar growled at her. "Bright red."

"You're indulging in rather a lot of attitude this evening," Milo observed calmly. He was very composed; they both were, actually. Elizabeth did not know how they had discharged their earlier anger, but it was entirely absent. She wasn't sure that was a good sign for her. "Remove your dress, princess," he repeated.

"Why? Do you want to wear it? Will you wear my dress and he my shoes?" She was far past the point of simple rudeness, but what did it matter now. "The two of you will not make very pretty sisters, but perhaps better ladies than kings."

Milo's calm might have been unassailable, but Ragnar's patience came to an abrupt and dramatic end. The barbarian laid hold of her, pulled her onto her stomach, and flipped the dress up over her head in one easy motion, revealing the length of her squirming thighs, the rounds of her bottom, the neat curve and flair of her hips. He wrapped his powerful palm around one calf and tugged the dress further, peeling it off her squirming body in one swift motion.

Now entirely naked, Elizabeth defended herself from punishment by hurling the first pillow that came to hand. It did very little to weaken Ragnar's grip on her leg, and absolutely nothing to stop the sudden sting that blazed across her ass as the sole of the slipper met her bottom. Elizabeth shrieked, took hold of another pillow and did her best to curl up on herself and beat Ragnar with the soft weapon. He still had hold of her leg, but she was able to twist and wield the pillow several times, a soft *flumph* sound emitting with every direct strike to his broad body.

"Unhand me, you vile barbarian!"

"Settle, princess," Milo censured her, snatching the

pillow from her hands. "You are being punished. I expect decorum from you."

Elizabeth stuck her tongue out and thumbed her nose. She owed these men no respect, no decorum, nothing at all. They would have to wrest submission from her, much like Milo had wrested the pillow.

Ragnar bought the slipper down twice more, once to each cheek. Even with relatively little force it stung like blazes. She would have kicked him if he didn't have one leg in his hand and if the other had not been tangled in the sheets of her bed. Even the furnishings were against her, so it seemed.

"Settle down," Milo said, clamping his large hand on the back of her neck. She was pinned against the bed, unable to move thanks to being held down by both of her lovers. In that position she was kept and spanked with the slipper well over a dozen more times, her flesh heated sharply with each and every slap.

She whimpered with the unfairness of it all. Did they truly expect her not to give them any resistance at all? Had her words been worthy of being held in place and punished like some errant maid? It was all deeply embarrassing for Elizabeth, from the indignity of her position, to the pain in her bottom, to the growing response between her thighs.

"You will speak respectfully," Milo lectured as Ragnar thrashed her. "You will mind your tongue and you will accept that there are consequences for disobedience. You are ours, princess, and we have expectations that will be enforced in ways you will not enjoy."

It was rather a redundant statement, given that her bottom was being soundly and relentlessly belabored with her own footwear by a barbarian more than twice her size.

"Naughty girl," Ragnar added, standing erect to survey the results of his handiwork. Elizabeth didn't know what her bottom looked like, but it felt hot and swollen and she could feel the sting somehow still singing on even though Ragnar had put the slipper down—and picked up the belt.

"No!" she squealed. "Not the belt!"

Ragnar doubled it over, snapping the leather against itself with a loud crack that made her cringe. His dark eyes were lit with purpose that would not bend to her pleas. Elizabeth reached back to cover her bottom with both hands and simultaneously squirmed up onto her knees so she could face them.

"This isn't fair," she said. "I mean, it's not, is it?" She looked at the two kings with a desperation in her eyes that did not do a thing to dissuade them. "What are you punishing me for? What did I do that was so wrong? I went to the market, I returned…"

"Bend over and present your bottom," Ragnar snapped.

She focused the entire intensity of her dismay upon him, her green eyes filling with tears. "Please… Ragnar… I have done all you asked of me."

"You have fought us from the moment we walked in here," Ragnar said mercilessly. "Bend over, princess."

"Very well," she said with a deep sigh. "I have no choice."

She hoped her feigned obedience would earn her some mercy as she turned around and bent over so that her bottom was high and her head was low.

The first crack of the belt against her bottom took her breath away. Ragnar wielded the thing with what felt like the full force of his arm and to Elizabeth's senses it was as if cannon fire had burst across her cheeks in a blazing salvo that made a cry burst forth from her lips.

He laid several more like it across her cheeks, striping from the top of her quivering bottom to the top of her thighs. She lost the ability to retain position within a stroke or two and thereafter simply writhed upon the bed, her legs scissoring and flailing in a futile attempt to discharge some of the heat and sting.

By the time Ragnar was done with her, her hips were dancing in desperate fashion, her pussy grinding against the bedding, not out of any arousal she was aware of, but out of necessity. The only way to escape the belt was to move away from it. The only way to move away from it was to press her squirming body against the bed.

"She's wet," Ragnar declared suddenly, tossing the belt to the side.

"Soaking," Milo agreed.

On the verge of real tears, Elizabeth was sure the both of them were utterly mad—until the barbarian ran his fingers between her thighs and she felt the slickness of her lower lips for herself as he thrust two thick digits deep into her clenching cunt.

"Oh, my…" Her fingers clutched at the sheets in erotic desperation as Ragnar pushed his fingers deep inside her and twisted them slowly, making the most of her wetness.

"She likes this too much," Ragnar said, talking to Milo almost as if Elizabeth were not even there, certainly as if her tender pussy were not stretched around his thick fingers. "This will not do. She will come and what will she learn?"

"Hold her there," Milo said. "I have something which will help."

Elizabeth was held there on the bed, squirming with a very sore bottom as Ragnar slowly pumped his fingers in and out of her. Milo was gone for several minutes, during with the barbarian seemed to lose patience with the wait. His fingers slid out of her body, his impressively powerful bulk eclipsed the light of the moon as he rose over her prone form, and his hard cock pushed deep into her tender depths in one long, mutually satisfying stroke.

She let out a gasp of pleasure pain, for her bottom was still very sore, but Ragnar's cock felt wonderful inside her.

"Don't you dare come, princess," he growled in her ear. "This is not for your pleasure."

It may not have been for her to enjoy, but there was no way Elizabeth could not feel good as his cock slowly sluiced in and out of her tight, wet cunt.

Milo re-entered the room just as Ragnar started to pick up the pace. He picked Elizabeth up too, denying her the chance to rub her clit against the bed. Instead he stood upright and fucked her facing away from his body, his strength impressive as he lifted her up and down on his thick root time and time again, displaying her to Milo as he did.

Elizabeth found herself moaning and writhing on Ragnar's cock as Milo gave her his sternest look, reminding her that this was punishment and she was not supposed to be getting pleasure out of it. He couldn't stop the way her body responded though. Her lower muscles were tightening, she could feel the tingling in her clit start to escalate, she was on the verge and...

Ragnar pulled her from his cock and set her on her knees on the bed, facing him.

"Open your mouth," Ragnar grunted.

Elizabeth did as she was told and he pushed his cock into her mouth, taking her head in his hands as he took the last few thrusts toward climax over her tongue and spilled his seed in several spurting torrents over the back of her tongue and down her throat.

She swallowed eagerly, her arousal making his cum taste delicious. Her pussy was wet and willing for more and she looked at Milo in the hopes that he would be overcome by his ardor and wish to take his turn.

Unfortunately, it was not so. He was holding something in his hands. Something shiny and made of metal, something...

"No!"

"Before you think of rubbing that little bud to climax when you are alone, this should remind you that you are being punished," Milo said firmly as he stepped forward and slid a silver belt about her waist.

It was made of a light chain mail that was about an inch wide. That was not too concerning alone, but the piece of molded silver on the front gave her more cause for concern as Milo pushed it between her thighs and fastened it at the back. She was now wearing a chastity belt.

"No," she said. "Please…"

"The next time you climax, it will be as a reward for good behavior," Milo informed her. "Now, go to bed and get some sleep. I will expect you to have a much more pleasant and considered demeanor in the morning."

Milo and Ragnar left her abruptly with her mouth still hanging open in surprise. She heard the door to her chamber lock from the outside. Elizabeth realized then that her plan could not have gone more awry if she had tried. Not only were Milo and Ragnar not at one another's throats, she was utterly alone, totally unsated, and wearing a piece of hardware that denied her access to her own genitals. Any one of those things alone would have disturbed her, but together they left her utterly infuriated.

She vowed vengeance on both of them, not just for spanking her so soundly, but for leaving her so wet and wanting. Ragnar had spilled his seed and taken his pleasure, but she was still burning with desire and there was no way to satisfy herself thanks to the metal ensconcing her mound.

But what could she do? What rebellion was possible when one was locked in a tower room with a chastity belt making finding her own climax impossible? She paced in circles, her ire rising with every circuit of the room… and then she remembered what she had forgotten. As the silver moon rose high in the sky, casting an ethereal light over her room, the vial still secreted in the folds of her day dress seemed to call her.

Elizabeth plucked it out between her fingers and held it up, the contents dark and mysterious. What was it the old woman had said about the brew? She could barely remember anymore. All she knew was that it was guaranteed to have some effect, and perhaps it would take the edge off her irritation. Milo and Ragnar had left her without so much as a drop of wine to sup upon. An argument could be made that she utterly had to drink the brew. It was the only logical thing to do.

With tentative fingers, she removed the cork stopper and

immediately thrust the little vial away from her. A pungent stench was emanating from it, something earthy and rotting and foul. Under any other circumstances, Elizabeth would never have considered drinking such a concoction, but this was her one opportunity for rebellion and she was motivated through sheer bloody mindedness to take it.

Pinching her nose with the fingers of one hand, she brought the vial to her lips. It was a very small amount of liquid, and if she drank it quickly enough she was sure she would not taste it at all. Gathering her courage, she tipped her head back and let the dark brew flow over her tongue.

That was a mistake. She should have tossed it all directly to the back of her throat. The taste was even worse than the smell, so much so that barely half of the vial made it down before the disgusting taste made her entire body shudder so forcefully that the vial fell from her fingers, shattered on the flagstone floor and cast the remnants of the liquid across the stone.

"Oh, my…" Elizabeth put her hands to her head. Already she did not feel well.

The effects seemed to compound on themselves by the second. Within minutes of drinking the brew her stomach was churning, her knees were weak, and her body was beginning to sweat from every pore. Elizabeth let out a groan as she collapsed onto her bed and began to writhe. Her mind was hazy, filled with disjointed thoughts and heated visions that made everything she looked at seem to swim and grow teeth. She looked out the window and did not see the moon, but rather a great silvery dragon with mouth open wide, poised to consume her entirely.

"Help!" she cried out in terror. "Help! I shall be eaten!"

The dragon drew back and then surged forward, lunging toward the window. All around her the walls seemed to shake and tremble, each of the flagstones of the floor were moving, sliding around one another in some great maze of motion her befuddled gaze could not begin to follow.

The bed was the only safe space in the room—until the

silken coverlets began to turn to water and she started to splash among them. There was something around her waist, she suddenly realized with a high-pitched shriek, something that seemed to be consuming her with great metal teeth...

• • • • • • •

When Elizabeth began to yell not a quarter hour after they had left her on her own, Milo's first impulse was to ignore her. She was trying to get his attention and he was quite determined that she should not have it. The spoiled princess needed to learn a lesson about who was in control and who was not.

He opened his door and stood in the hall, listening. Ragnar came up the stairs and did much the same thing.

*"Help! I am dying! I am done for! I am already dead!"*

"Either she is actually dying, or she is the best actress in Ammerdale," Ragnar growled, starting for the door. Milo followed in his wake, quite concerned by the desperation in her cries.

It was Ragnar who burst through the door first, Milo following after him. They found Elizabeth quite delirious, tossing and turning on the bed. The sheets were sticking to her with the excess perspiration, winding about her limbs and increasing her panic as she flailed at her waist.

"It's eating me! The dragon has me in its mouth! It has me!"

Her fingers were red from scrabbling at the chastity belt, which she had clearly mistaken for some kind of voracious creature.

"Shhhh..." Milo went to her side. She looked at him with glassy, unfocused eyes.

"A golden angel! Save me, golden angel!" She clutched at him most desperately and implored him for help from the very bottom of her soul.

"She is ill," Milo said grimly as he began to remove the belt that was causing her such distress. "Shhh, princess. I am taking it off."

"The dragon ate half of me!" Elizabeth cried. "The good half!"

"Shhhh," Milo repeated, attempting to calm her. "You are in one piece, lie still now."

"I cannot! I will drown!"

Her cries would have been comical if she were not so distressed. She had utterly lost touch with the reality of the world about her. Milo had never seen a person so very ill before. Seeing Elizabeth in such a state disturbed him to his very core. He did not know what to do with the writhing young lady who seemed to be so ill. In that moment he would have given anything to have her back to her old insolent self.

"There are little dragons swimming in the water," Elizabeth burbled. "Or are they crocodiles? Will they smile at me? Do not smile, crocodiles, I do not trust you at all."

• • • • • • •

That Elizabeth had fallen ill was obvious. What was not so obvious was why. Ragnar was far more interested in that than in attending to the princess' complaints about dragons and such. She was completely out of her mind, and Ragnar knew that kind of disturbance of the mind did not happen without some cause.

While Milo attended to the princess, Ragnar scanned the room for any signs of an assailant. The state Elizabeth was in did not have the marks of a natural illness. Something else was afoot, he was sure of it. In very quick order, he saw a dark stain upon the floor and went to his knees beside it, his head down as he sniffed a familiar scent.

"Have a bath drawn," Ragnar said. "I have seen this before. She has a poison of sorts."

"She has been poisoned? By who?"

"Most likely by herself," Ragnar said. "I know the smell of it anywhere. What she drank is a distilled brew of vines and lichens. It is powerful." He scooped Elizabeth's quivering form up from the bed, meaning to carry her to the bath chamber.

"Hot water and plenty of it!" He barked the order at Milo, who was looking utterly stricken. "And salts! As many salts as can be gathered!"

Milo stared at him and Elizabeth, until Ragnar boomed on the verge of fury, "Go! Now!"

The roared order snapped Milo out of his panic and sent him to carry out the necessary preparations. Ragnar turned his attention back to the princess, who was shaking in his arms, moaning and muttering all sorts of nonsense.

It took some time for the bath to be prepared the way Ragnar instructed it to be. It took a chain of maids to bring buckets of water to the tub, and then a squire to bring a large bag of salts and dissolve it into the bathwater. The castle was a lit with tension and concern, for not one person within it wished any ill upon Elizabeth. She had been a popular figure for a very long time among those who had served under her father, and even the newer members serving under Milo and Ragnar felt a fondness for her.

When the water was ready, Ragnar gently lowered her into the bath. While in his arms, she had settled a great deal. The visions that had been plaguing her had either subsided, or drawn her deeper into herself.

"She is sweating, should she not be in a cool bath?" Milo had been pacing about the bath chamber the entire time and still his legs were wearing the same path as Ragnar ensured that Elizabeth was in no danger of slipping below the waterline. Her muscles were not entirely under her control, and she certainly didn't have the mental ability to keep herself safe in that moment.

"She is not sweating from fever," Ragnar said. "What she has taken makes all the body's functions work faster and harder. The hot water and salt will leech some of the brew from her body. The heat will soothe her muscles and make the visions fade."

"Are you sure?" Milo pushed both his hands through his pale hair in a gesture of helpless concern.

"I am very sure," Ragnar assured Milo. He had never before seen the man look so worried. It was a strange thing to see pain and fear written on the brave young king's face. Ragnar did not have time to attend to Milo in the moment, however; it was more important to ensure that Elizabeth was held with her head above the water as her racked body adjusted to the heat of the bath.

Almost immediately upon becoming immersed, the physical tremors had begun to subside. The contortions of her face were not so extreme either, the expressions of pain and fear fading into a more composed expression.

"How do you know what to do?"

"They call it Seer's Spawn," Ragnar said. "It's dangerous, but I do not think she has taken enough to die."

"You don't think!" Milo raised his hands high above his head and his eyes rolled. "What do you mean you don't think!?"

"Calm down, pup," Ragnar growled. "She is already responding to the treatment and she has purged most of it already, I am sure. All we can do now is wait for the brew to take its course."

Milo's shoulders drooped in defeat as he walked to sit on the side of the tub and gaze down at Elizabeth with a sad expression. "Have we been so cruel to her, Ragnar? Why would she do this?"

"When my warriors do it, it is in search of a vision ordeal," Ragnar said, sponging the water over her forehead. "She will be ill for many hours. It will be dawn before the effects wear thin and we might see what damage has been done to her."

"We did this to her," Milo frowned. "We let her out into the public sphere. We left her alone…"

"She is young," Ragnar reminded him. "In my lands, it is not uncommon for a young man or woman to find a substance of interest and imbibe more than is good for the body or the soul. Are things not so in the north?"

Milo gave a small shrug. "We have brews, of course," he said. "Wine, mead, heavier stout. One may drink too much, but the results are rarely so intense."

"No fungi? No variants of tobacco?"

"They do not grow in northern climes."

"Then you have much to learn about the bounties of nature," Ragnar chuckled. He was quite confident now that Elizabeth would come to no lasting harm. Her tremors had ceased almost completely and her shoulders were quite relaxed against his arm. It was easy to hold her there in the bath and occasionally swirl a little water around her to encourage the salt to do its work.

"How can you laugh at a time like this?" Milo's eyes narrowed with fury. "We could have lost her. Do you not care?"

"We have not lost her," Ragnar replied calmly. "I do enjoy seeing the calculating boy king concerned for once. You are usually so full of yourself."

"Do not call me a boy king," Milo growled. "I am right to be concerned. Lichens and vines? She has taken poison. She could have died."

"She could have, perhaps, if she had taken a great deal more," Ragnar admitted. "But it is also true that she could drown in this bath, if it were as large as the ocean. There is no sense in worrying about that which has not happened."

Milo nodded, though he did not seem overly convinced. "So you think she took it to escape her woes?"

"I do not know why she took it," Ragnar replied. "All I know is that she will not be harmed."

Milo took a deep breath and let it out in a sigh. "Very well," he said, wringing his hands. "I have to trust your judgment." He slid down to the floor next to the tub and sat with his knees drawn up to his chest.

"This will be a long vigil," Ragnar reminded him. "Go and rest."

"I will not leave her side," Milo said determinedly. "You

may need my help."

There was no convincing Milo to leave, and there was no point in it either, so Ragnar let the topic go and soon they lapsed into silence. The hour was very late and they were all tired. Ragnar's warrior training meant that he was used to staying up through the night. Milo was used to formal patrols, ordered soldiers, a systemic hierarchy that allowed the king some rest. Ragnar's life had not been so fortunate or so easy. Hardship had marked each and every year, but made him stronger in the process. So it was that he took the night vigil.

Soon enough, Milo lost the battle with sleep and ended up curled against the tub, his arm stretched along the lip of it, his head resting on his arm. Ragnar had not felt much in the way of goodwill toward the younger king until that very moment, and perhaps it was only his own exhaustion and the affection he felt for Elizabeth confusing his responses, but he felt a measure of protectiveness over and even pride in Milo. He couldn't quite place why he felt those things, except, perhaps, for the fact that they were becoming a little family, the three of them.

There was a quiet sloshing as Elizabeth came to in the bath. The water had been cooling for some time and her consciousness was probably a function of becoming uncomfortable. He was still holding her as she opened her eyes and spoke softly.

"Hello."

"Hello, princess," he rumbled gently. "Back in the world of the living."

"I have seen… everything," she said softly, her eyes closing once more.

"I am sure you have," he chuckled softly. He had drunk the brew himself in his younger years many times under the guidance of the shaman. The visions were still with him in the recesses of his mind. Elizabeth would not soon forget her evening, of that he was absolutely certain. "Time to get out of the bath, princess," he murmured. "We don't want you getting all wrinkly."

"I am a wrinkle," she said in the same soft tones as he lifted her out of the water and set her upon his knee to dry her off. She was physically much better, but mentally she was still barely coherent, half in the world of the living, half in the world beyond. Ragnar kept the motion of his towel slow and soothing so as not to disturb her in her visions. Best to let them run their course.

When she was dry, he took her back to her bed and laid down with her. She curled up next to him, her fingers curling in the hair of his chest.

"You are furry," she intoned. "You are an animal man."

"Aren't we all?" He took her hand and gently guided it down between her thighs to where the bush of bright red hair was still slightly damp.

"I am an animal woman," she said in wondrous tones. "I can hunt and bite and burrow…"

"You can do all of that tomorrow," Ragnar replied. "For the moment, you need only sleep."

"Yes," she said as her eyes closed again. "Sleep."

# CHAPTER EIGHT

In the very early hours of the morning, Milo woke with a sore neck from sleeping cramped between tub and floor. Neither Ragnar nor Elizabeth were there when he roused himself. With aching muscles, he stood up and stretched, getting blood back into parts of his body that were tingling with pins and needles for having missed it. His left leg particularly was suffering so he limped somewhat painfully into Elizabeth's chamber, where he found both Ragnar and Elizabeth in bed. She was sleeping very peacefully, so it seemed. Her cheeks were a good color and her breath was coming evenly. She looked well. A great rushing sensation of relief went coursing through his body.

He had never loved before. He knew that only now that he had contemplated Elizabeth's loss and found himself almost paralyzed as a result. In the past there had been dalliances with pretty courtesans and the daughters of hopeful noblemen. Many he had been fond of, but his affection for Elizabeth was very different. Thinking about losing her was like thinking about losing the very core of his soul.

Milo cleared his throat and a moment later, Ragnar's eyes opened. He put a finger to his lips and gently disentangled himself from Elizabeth, who made a small sound of complaint in her sleep, but soon settled into the pillows and blankets and was softly snoring as Ragnar and Milo stepped out of the room to talk.

"See? She is well," Ragnar said with a laugh. "No need to look so concerned."

"She looks much improved," Milo agreed. "Thank you for looking after her... for all you did last night. I was of little use, I confess. If it had not been for you, I would not have known what to do. She might have suffered more, she might possibly have perished..."

"She would have come around," Ragnar assured him. "Worse for wear, but the dose was not fatal."

The news did not make Milo feel any better. The dose could very well have been fatal for all he knew. And the fact that she seemed to be well now did not shed any light on the reason why she had taken the brew in the first place.

"Where did she get it? Was she trying to harm herself? Did she say anything to you?"

"She said very little to me in the night," Ragnar said. "And what she did say made little sense. That is the way of the brew. Now she likely has her senses back, we can try to get some coherent answers from her."

"Yes," Milo said grimly. "Let us do that. Let us do that now."

• • • • • • •

So it was that Elizabeth woke with a pounding headache and the faces of two very stern men looking down at her.

"Ugh," she moaned. "What happened?"

"That's for you to answer, princess." Milo's tone was stern and snappy. He was certainly not happy with something, though Elizabeth was sure she did not know what. Her mind was remarkably devoid of thoughts at first. She looked at Ragnar, who was smirking in a way that seemed to imply some sort of paternalistic amusement at the situation.

There was a clue somewhere in his visage and suddenly the memory came back. The little vial, the pungent liquid she'd choked down… and then everything else. She felt very sore and very, very foolish. She did not entirely know what had happened in the hours between taking the brew and waking in the bed. Her memories were jumbled and fantastic, dreamlike in their consistency, or lack thereof.

"I swam in a warm lake…"

"You were in the bath," Ragnar said with a snort of amusement.

Elizabeth blinked, trying to discern what was real from that which was not. Her mind was full of memories that seemed half real and yet could not possibly have been real: a dragon that coiled like a serpent around the tower, being bathed by a burly barbarian, and a golden-haired sorrowful angel that hovered about crying great tears.

"You drank something last night," Ragnar said calmly. "Where did you get it?"

She felt a tightening in her chest. How did he know what she had done? Had she somehow told him in her delirium?

"I didn't drink anything…"

Ragnar fixed her with his dark, intense gaze. "Now is not the time to lie, princess."

The words were delivered softly, but with a weight that made her tremble. She looked over at Milo and saw nothing but sorrow and perhaps disappointment in his blue eyes.

"Where did you get the brew?"

"In the market…" She made the admission very sheepishly.

"Did you know what it was when you bought it?"

"No, I didn't intend to buy it. I paid someone to tell my future and they gave it to me."

"Who?"

"I don't know. She was old. An old woman. She wanted to talk to me and she said that if I drank the drink I would learn all about the future. I would see everything. She said I would find the truth…" Elizabeth would have explained more, but she was brusquely interrupted.

"To take an unknown liquid from a stranger in a market, and to drink it… do you lack all forms of the most common sense?" Milo's tongue lashed her, his hands on his hips, his eyes narrowed with what felt to Elizabeth like real anger.

"Says the man who locked my womanhood behind a quarter inch of steel," Elizabeth shot back. "What sense is there in my life?"

Milo and Elizabeth glared at one another, each quite furious.

"You will never go out unattended again," Milo vowed. "You will be fortunate to see the outside of this room."

"Calm yourself," Ragnar interjected as Elizabeth drew in a deep breath with which to express her vehement dismay. "She made a mistake. There is nothing to be gained from keeping her in a tower for the rest of her life."

"I will not calm myself," Milo replied. "She was utterly delirious. She was deeply ill. And if she goes about drinking anything that is presented to her, she will die long before her time is due. And to do it because she was punished…"

Elizabeth did not hear the rest of Milo's words, for Ragnar had taken hold of Milo and dragged him bodily out of the room.

· · · · · · ·

"Stop it," Ragnar scowled down at Milo.

Milo was not in the mood to be told what to do, especially not by Ragnar. "You're undermining me," he complained bitterly.

"You're overreacting," Ragnar replied. "You want a bond with her, do you not? You will never achieve it if all you do is scold and punish. She drank the brew after we thrashed and fucked her and put her in a belt. Harsh treatment only goes so far. She knows she made a mistake. She knows she has more punishment due too. But you must get control of your temper before that happens."

Milo knew Ragnar was right. He didn't want to know it, but good sense penetrated his anger anyway. He took a deep breath and sighed to himself.

"Since when did you become the voice of reason?"

"Since you lost your mind with fear when you saw her ill," Ragnar replied. "Go to the stables, take your favorite horse, and ride out for the day. You need to clear your head."

Milo looked at him with suspicion. At no time since the capture of the castle had either of them left the grounds—and for good reason. If one left, there was the chance the other could fortify and make it impossible for the other to return. Possession was the only way to maintain control. Ragnar was boldly suggesting that Milo trust him not just with the castle, but with the princess.

"We cannot all three of us be imprisoned here forever," Ragnar pointed out. "You have my word I will not make off with her. You are becoming maddened by confinement. Much like she was."

"Very well," Milo agreed. "I will clear my head and I will deal with her later."

"You may deal with what is left of her," Ragnar said. "Believe me when I tell you that the princess will be getting her comeuppance."

It was somewhat mollifying to know that Elizabeth would be disciplined immediately. Milo was truly furious with her, not just because of her reckless actions, but because of her total lack of concern. It was as if she did not know what danger was. She was so sheltered, so very naive.

"Go," Ragnar said, patting his shoulder. "She's safe with me."

• • • • • • •

While the men argued in muffled voices outside her door, Elizabeth sat most worried for her rear and other parts of her anatomy. She had never seen Milo so incensed—so much so that the barbarian had been the one to tell him to calm down. What would Milo do to her? She sat up with her thighs squeezed tight together, her knees pressed against her chest and her arms locked around them, nervously staring at the door, waiting for the men to come back.

When only Ragnar returned, she felt a tangible sense of relief.

"Where is Milo?"

"Clearing his head," Ragnar said, settling into the chair next to the bed. He stretched his long legs out in front of himself and looked at her with a fairly neutral expression.

"I did not know one could clear that which is already empty," Elizabeth said pertly.

Ragnar snorted and shook his head. "He is worried about you."

"He is angry at me."

"He is both," Ragnar said.

"But you're not." She cocked her head and looked at him with a mischievous smile. "Is that because you weren't worried?"

"It's because I know exactly what you took, and because I know exactly what I'm going to do to make sure you don't ever do anything so stupid again."

The grin fell right off her face.

"My words have some effect," Ragnar said. "Good. But words are just the beginning. I held you through the night. Made sure you were safe…"

"Thank you," Elizabeth interrupted him, heartfelt emotion in the words. "Really, I mean it. I know I was foolish…"

"You didn't know what you were drinking. You didn't know the person you got it from. You were more interested in petulant act of disobedience than in your own well-being. Are you so eager to escape us that you are willing to die a painful, poisonous death?"

"No," she answered in a small, soft, very guilty voice. "I didn't think…"

"That's exactly right," Ragnar interjected. "You didn't think. You didn't think when a stranger approached you in the market. You didn't think when you kept that a secret from us. And you definitely didn't think when you drank it. This wasn't one lapse in good judgment, princess. You haven't shown any kind of sense since this began. You are far more concerned with rebellion."

"You sound like Milo."

"Milo was right," Ragnar said gruffly. "Now come here, lay yourself over my thighs, and take the spanking you are due."

• • • • • • •

Elizabeth looked incredibly sheepish, but to her credit, she did as she was told. She slid her naked body off the bed and came to lay across his thighs. Ragnar patted her bottom, enjoying the way his palm covered her cheek entirely. She was a beautiful young woman, a spirited one too. If she had been born a barbarian, she might have made an excellent huntress. As a princess, she was perhaps ill-suited to her confinement.

He began to spank her, keeping his word to Milo and his promise to Elizabeth too. The slaps were firm and swift, covering her bottom in a barrage that turned pale cheeks pink. She let out plaintive squeaks that were rather adorable and that might have softened his resolve if it weren't for the fact she could have just as easily have drunk hemlock as vision brew.

"I'm sorry, Ragnar!" She made another impassioned appeal just as her bottom started to go a brighter shade of red. "Really, I am truly sorry. I was stupid. I know that. Truly I do."

He had never heard her apologize for anything so much. That fact made him slow his slaps and speak to her instead.

"You have to promise me you will never do anything like this again," he said. "If you want to drink something, you must show me it first."

"I promise!" Elizabeth gasped. "It was terrible. It was frightening! I will never do anything like it again, I truly, truly, truly promise!"

Her cheeks were not as red as they could have been, but truth be told Ragnar did not have it in his heart to thrash her too severely. He knew all too well that the effects of the brew were in many respects their own punishment. Milo's anger seemed to have chastised her greatly as well.

In spite of himself, Ragnar found his palm stroking her bottom instead of spanking it, and then he pulled her up so she could sit on his lap. She rewarded him for his kindness by nuzzling against his bearded face.

"You will tell him, won't you," she said hopefully. "You will tell him that you already punished me and that I have learned my lesson."

"He will make his own decision when he speaks with you," Ragnar said. "I would not count on him to be as lenient as I have been."

"But that's not fair, to be punished twice."

"You answer to two kings, Elizabeth," he said. "It may not be fair, but I think you know you have been fortunate with me. Be grateful for that at least. I barely punished you at all."

"Thank you," she said, pressing a kiss to his cheek. In spite of himself, Ragnar could not help the smile that rose to his lips. She was a naughty little minx, but she was his naughty little minx.

# CHAPTER NINE

Milo did not return that night. Nor was he back the next day.

Elizabeth noticed his absence and remarked that he must be terribly angry with her to stay away for so long. Ragnar assured her that it was not anger that kept Milo away, but when she inquired as to the reason for his absence, Ragnar did not have an answer.

"It is my fault," she said sadly, gazing out the window. "You saw how very angry he was with me. And with you... he was furious with the both of us. Perhaps he has decided he no longer wants the kingdom, or me."

She was convinced, but Ragnar was not nearly so certain that the reason for Milo's continued absence had anything to do with Elizabeth. He privately sent several patrols in search of the king, but they returned with little in the way of information. Nobody had seen Milo, none of the peasants tilling the fields, and there was no sign of him or his horse.

As the day wore on and night fell and another day began, Elizabeth began to become quite withdrawn. Her mood was the least of Ragnar's problems, however. Milo's men were starting to become restless. There were whispers of foul play. The camaraderie that had been building between

Ragnar's forces and Milo's men started to deteriorate as rumors swirled and became stronger.

It became clear to Ragnar that he was going to have to find Milo one way or another. It was equally obvious that Elizabeth would have to come with him. He could not risk letting her out of his sight, in case Milo's disappearance was the result of foul play.

Having marshaled his men into three search parties, he made his way to the tower where Elizabeth was lying on her bed, moping for her lost lover. She turned toward Ragnar as he entered, wiping her reddened eyes. Her sorrow was so great it seemed to fill the entire room.

"Come, princess," he said. "We are going in search of Milo."

"Oh," she said, suddenly looking as though she were holding back a vast sea of tears. "Good luck. I will not say farewell, for I will likely lose you both."

"You do not understand," Ragnar said. "We are going in search of Milo. You as well as I."

His words were apparently so strange to her ears that she was not sure she had heard them at all. "We are?"

"I will not leave you here alone," Ragnar said. "I need my eyes on you. So you will ride with me and my men and together we will find King Lionheart."

"Will I be in danger?"

Ragnar looked at her with an intensity in his dark gaze that gave his words additional weight. "I will not allow danger to so much as breathe on you."

A smile broke across her pretty face. "Let us go find Milo."

She did not know what she was getting into, and Ragnar did not have time to let her know. He put her on a horse and told her to follow directly in his wake at all times.

"I should have a weapon," she said as they rode out of the city.

"You don't need a weapon. You have me," he replied over his shoulder. Elizabeth grinned, looking tremendously pretty in the sunshine. She was wearing a simple green robe that emphasized her red hair and emerald eyes and had he not been on a serious mission, Ragnar would have loved nothing more than to take her in his arms and make love to her.

As it was, he had to command the men to spread out and search. There were valleys, forests, and little hamlets spread out around Ammerdale City, and Milo could be hidden away almost anywhere. Privately, Ragnar was concerned that Milo might already be dead. It was not in his nature to flee, and though he had been frustrated with Elizabeth, there was no chance he had left her.

Ragnar elected to search the forest with Elizabeth in tow. It was perhaps something of a risk, but his men were in earshot and he had his horn, which he could blow if he were to need help. The more of the land they could cover, the better.

For hours they rode through underbrush, horses plodding slowly as they scoured the countryside. It was difficult, tedious work, and he was proud of how well Elizabeth handled it, though she was hardly used to spending time in the saddle.

"There!"

Her sharp eyes had spotted a small scrap of red cloth fluttering against a thorn.

"Excellent spotting, princess," Ragnar said, spurring his horse toward a trail that was largely obscured by a great vine and bush. He would have missed it entirely if it were not for her shout. The trail went on for a mile or so through dense forest, then emerged into a clearing where the remnants of a camp were obvious in the form of middens of discarded food scraps, the charred remains of a fire—and a man tied to a tree.

Milo.

Ragnar barely recognized him at first. His clothing was filthy and tattered and his blond shock of hair was matted with earth and other filth to the point it no longer looked blond. His head hung down against his chest in an unconscious pose. He was held upright by ropes wrapped around his torso, arms, and legs, which bound him to the trunk of the tree. It was immediately obvious that he had been beaten. There was dried blood beneath his nose and bruising around his eyes.

Elizabeth let out a gasp of shock and horror. She slid from the horse, ran to him, and wrapped her arms around him as delicately as she could. Milo let out a cry of surprise as he came to consciousness.

"Milo! What have they done to you?"

"It's alright," he reassured her. "I am... well. No real harm has come to me."

"It's my fault, isn't it! I made you angry and you left and..."

"Move aside, princess," Ragnar said. "I must cut him down."

Ragnar bought a sharp knife down against the ropes, sawing at the bonds that kept Milo in place. As the ropes fell away, Milo's muscles failed him. He collapsed into the leaf litter of the forest floor, to Elizabeth's shrieked dismay. Ragnar came back around the tree and hauled Milo up to his feet, half-carried and half-walked him to the horse.

The steed stood obligingly still as Ragnar hoisted Milo up and into the saddle. Milo did his best to hold himself erect upon the horse, but it was obvious that he was in pain and he soon slumped forward against the horse's neck.

"Who did this?" It was Elizabeth who asked the question. Ragnar could see his anger reflected in her pretty face. She was most disturbed by what she had seen, and he wished she had not seen it. She had the stricken expression of someone who had finally understood an aspect of humanity that had escaped her throughout long years of enforced innocence.

"He needs water," Ragnar explained. "Questions later. Water now." He held the water skin up to Milo's lips and the king gratefully took a few sips. He looked utterly exhausted, and Ragnar could see the effects of several beatings upon the man. Anger rose in him, a fury that somebody had dared attack his ally. It was an act of disrespect, not just toward Milo, but toward him as well.

"I didn't think you'd come." The words were directed at Ragnar.

"Of course I came," Ragnar replied. "We have an alliance."

"We have an alliance," Milo nodded, his voice rasping.

"Your voice sounds so strange," Elizabeth said. "The cool night air must have made your throat sore."

Ragnar knew very well that Milo did not have a sore throat from a cold night. His was the voice of a man who had yelled and screamed for hours. He could only imagine what must have been inflicted on him to produce such a result.

He ended up having to strap Milo into place on the horse. The man's muscles were weakened by exposure and dehydration and lack of food. He and Elizabeth rode on the second, fresher horse, keeping Milo's steed tied to theirs.

Ragnar blew his horn three times and the patrols he had sent out to patrol around the area met them as they emerged from the clearing and together they all rode back to the castle, where they were met with much concern and interest from all parties. Milo had not long been a presence, but he had gained loyalty from more than his own men. Ragnar noticed that several of the barbarian troops made it a point to ensure that the king was alive, and seemed glad to see that it was so.

Elizabeth refused to leave Milo's side as he was carried into the fortified tower and taken to the physician's chamber. There were two men in residence there; one who had provided services to Milo's army, the other to Ragnar's. Both looked grim as Milo was carried into their presence, his face an ashen gray pallor.

"You go no further," Ragnar said, barring Elizabeth's way. "The medicine men need to attend to him."

"I don't want to leave him," she pouted.

"He needs to rest," Ragnar said firmly. "You will see him tomorrow. The physician will sedate him, there is nothing you can do now."

"But…"

Ragnar took hold of Elizabeth by the shoulders and spoke calmly, but firmly. "I need your obedience now, princess," he said. "As does Milo. He is quite ill and suffering with his wounds. You can best help him by letting the physicians do their work without interruption."

She nodded slowly. "Very well," she said. "But I wish to see him tomorrow."

"Tomorrow," Ragnar agreed. He turned her around and sent her toward her chamber with a swat to her bottom before going into the physician's chamber himself. The heavy oak door had hidden the gasping and growling between clenched teeth, wounded animal noises emanating from the young king as the physicians tended to the marks on Milo's body. There were lacerations and seared marks, an array of unpleasant wounds inflicted in a deliberate nature that made Ragnar's fury simmer.

Milo gave him a wan smile as he entered the room. He had the flushed appearance of a man who had been given a sedating brew and who would soon be entirely off his gourd.

"She wants to see you," Ragnar said. "I have managed to put her off until tomorrow."

"Thank you," Milo said. "For saving my reputation before Elizabeth. I would not have her see me like this. She has seen too much already. I wish she had not been with you when I was found."

"She was only concerned for you," Ragnar said. "She missed you terribly. I faced a mutiny from your men and from her."

"Ah," Milo said through cracked lips. "So that was why you came for me. To avoid mutiny."

"I came for you because we have a pact," Ragnar growled in friendly fashion. "I don't leave my allies to suffer or fall. I would have thought you would have a guard with you. Why did you ride out without one?"

"I wanted to be alone," Milo said. "My thoughts were confused. They are not anymore."

"Good. We will need to be single-minded to deal with those who…"

He was interrupted by the opening of the door and the fast scurrying of Elizabeth's feet as she utterly disregarded their agreement and ran to Milo's side, bursting into great sobs as she did.

"I am sorry!" Tears flowed from Elizabeth's eyes profusely as she went to her knees next to Milo. "It was all my fault. I was bad and I made you leave…"

"It was not your fault," Milo reassured her. "What happened had nothing to do with you…"

Misery was still written all over her face in spite of his reassurances. "I made you angry and you left, and then someone did this to you."

"I am a king who has just made a conquest, Elizabeth. The world is full of people who would do this and worse if they were to have the chance. It was my fault I did not take an adequate guard." He reached out and put a hand on her head as she bowed it and cried profusely into the bed.

Ragnar could see the effort even the small motion took Milo. He reached out, took Elizabeth under her arms, and drew her up to her feet.

"You have seen him now," he said. "And you see he needs rest. Will you let him rest now?"

"I will," she sobbed. "I just want to know who did this."

Ragnar glanced at Milo. He also wanted to know who was responsible, but debriefing a man in as much pain as Milo was in was quite often pointless. The physicians would have given him a brew to make him relax and to stifle some of the pain, and even if they had not, the discomfort would lessen his ability to make sense. He needed rest, and plenty of it.

"We will find out in due course," he told Elizabeth.

"Now give the man his rest."

"No," Milo grunted. "She can stay. I know… who did this. They expected me to die. They spoke carelessly toward the end."

"Who?" The question came from Ragnar and Elizabeth at once.

"A general named Gusig. He wishes to marry Elizabeth."

"Gusig!" Elizabeth screwed her face up in true disgust. "He is foul. I would not marry him if there were no more men left in all the world."

"Who is he?"

"He was once one of my father's generals," Elizabeth said. "He fled before my father's death. He must have taken some of the soldiers with him…" She sighed. "We have lost track of many of the old guard. In the final months, my father was unable to command. The armies were splintered, under attack from every corner…" She cast a faintly reproachful look at Ragnar as she spoke.

Ragnar knew very well that it was his and Milo's actions that had been to blame. No war was ever without consequences, no conquest ever so complete that all resistance was eliminated on the first pass. He was not surprised that there was an old general with designs upon the crown. He was surprised that the man had been so brazen and so brutal as to attack Milo and subject him to such cruel treatment. It was an opportunistic, sadistic act that would be paid for many times over.

"He is disgusting," Elizabeth repeated. "I will not marry him, I will not!"

"You are ours," Ragnar reminded her. "He is nothing more than a coward who will regret the day he dared order his men lay hands on one of our number. I will have his head, and the blood of every man who was involved."

• • • • • • •

Ragnar looked as fierce in that moment as Elizabeth had ever seen him. She felt a shiver of fear and admiration rush through her belly and settle low in her abdomen. It was exciting to see him in the state that would have struck terror into anyone who would dare oppose him. She could not imagine an old braggart like Gusig being able to stand up to Ragnar for a moment.

She could barely stand to look at Milo. He had always been so handsome and proud, but in that moment he was so hurt, so wounded that he seemed much younger than his years. She wanted desperately to comfort him, to wrap her arms around him and hold him tight, but everything seemed to cause him pain.

"May I wash his face?" She addressed the question to the physician. "I must help in some way."

She took the bowl of warm water and the cloth and gently began to clean the streaks of mud and blood from Milo's visage. His eyes were closed now, his breathing even. The brew that he had been given was taking full effect and she was glad for it.

"He suffered greatly for me," she murmured.

"Yes," Ragnar agreed.

"Will he heal?"

"Yes," Ragnar said yet again. He had always been a man of relatively few words, but he had become almost monosyllabic. She turned to look at him with an inquiring expression and saw a look of fierce tenderness on his face. His great bush brows were drawn down low over his expressive brown eyes. His large, muscular arms were resting upon his knees as he sat watching over the pair of them, a sad sentinel.

"Why do you look so miserable?"

"The invasion was easy," Ragnar said. "I alone was king. I had no care besides that of taking what I could. And now I find myself the lover of a princess and protector of a kingdom three times greater than before. I find myself allied with another man. I find myself..." His words dwindled until Elizabeth bought them forth in her own tongue.

"You find yourself with people to care about. Perhaps to love. I think you love Milo as much as you love me."

"Differently," he said in a gruff admission, which made her smile.

"So you do love me," she said, her smile growing broader.

"Of course." He spoke as if it had never been in question. Elizabeth turned back to Milo, brushing some of his blond hair from his face. She had sponged some of it clean, but he would need a bath to wash it properly. She was much like Ragnar, she supposed. She had never had anyone to look after before, but suddenly she found herself feeling very protective over her wounded king. It was strange, how less than a month earlier she had not known either man except by reputation, and now she could not fathom the idea of a life without either one of them.

# CHAPTER TEN

Milo recovered from his injuries quickly, though Ragnar insisted that he was not giving himself proper time to heal and kept insisting that he rest. That did not please Milo, whose regal temperament was not given to taking orders, especially not from another king.

"I have told you a hundred times, I am well!" His words might have carried more weight had he not been visibly limping under the weight of his armor. He had made an appearance at one of the regular training sessions, intending on taking part. Ragnar was not allowing it.

"You are not well," Ragnar replied. "Your ribs are still healing and you swig brew hourly to keep the pain of the other wounds at bay. I know what a man struggling to keep up with his unit looks like. There is a time to be brave, and there is a time to admit that you have been harmed. Go and heal properly."

Milo's temper flared. He hated being weak. He hated seeing pity in Ragnar's eyes even more.

"You think that if it were you, they would not have taken you," he said. "You think you are stronger than I, don't you?"

"I did not say that."

"No, but you think it." Milo's blue eyes blazed. "I was not weak, Ragnar."

"I know you weren't," Ragnar growled back. "What will it take to convince you?"

"You can stop pitying me and fussing like an old woman. You are worse than Elizabeth!"

"How is he worse than I?" Elizabeth appeared on the scene with an expression almost more fearsome than Ragnar's. "What are you saying about me?"

"I am not saying a thing about you," Milo said. "I am saying Ragnar is acting like a woman."

He had hoped his words would mollify Elizabeth. Instead, they annoyed both Elizabeth and Ragnar.

"You're the one acting like a girl," Elizabeth shot back. "Refusing to do as the physicians say. If I did that, I'd be in trouble. Big trouble."

"You would be," Milo agreed.

"It's not fair to hold me to a standard you don't keep, is it?"

"No," Milo admitted.

"Then go to my bedchamber," Elizabeth said, pointing imperiously. "You have been naughty and I must punish you!"

She had an adorably serious expression on her face, so much so that Milo could not maintain his self-obsession and pity any longer.

"Well, Ragnar," he said. "I have been summoned, and I suppose I must obey."

"Better you do," Ragnar agreed.

Milo followed Elizabeth to her tower chamber, where she ordered him to lie on the bed. After removing his armor, he did so, lying on his back. She crawled onto the bed and looked down at him with her playfully stern expression.

"I will not spank you," she said magnanimously, "because I am much nicer than you are."

"Oh, is that so?" Milo grinned. The pain of his wounds truly was much abated for spending time with her. "What will you do, in that case?"

"I will lecture you," she said, her chin lifted as she looked down at him with hooded eyes. "You have been a very naughty king."

"Have I now?"

"Yes," she scowled. "You got hurt and now you insist on going about trying to fight everything before your wounds are healed. You deserve a good thrashing!"

There was real hurt behind her words. He could hear it in her voice, and it made him feel rather guilty. It had not occurred to him that his resistance to rest was causing Elizabeth real distress, and making the original fright she'd gotten at seeing him wounded so much worse.

"That was a very good lecture, princess," he praised. He grabbed her and pulled her down next to him, pressing a kiss to her cheek. She giggled and did not put up much in the way of resistance, seeming content to press against him and drink in his scent with deep breaths.

He closed his eyes and she closed hers and together they drifted into a much needed nap. They had both been through a great deal. He physically, her emotionally, and sleep was the best medicine for them both. Night had fallen by the time they woke up, and judging by the position of the moon, they had been asleep for four or five hours. The castle seemed uniquely quiet to Milo as he opened his eyes and gazed down at Elizabeth's beauty.

She stirred not long after, perhaps sensing his wakefulness in some fashion. Her eyes opened and she looked up at him with a gaze that was as earnest as it was loving.

"Don't ever leave like that again," she said in soft tones that brought tears to his eyes. "I was so worried about you."

"We may have to leave to fight this general, Ragnar and I."

"No!" She sat up, an angry look on her pretty face. "I forbid either of you to leave my side!"

He reached up and tenderly brushed fiery strands of hair

out of her eyes. "We must lead our armies, Elizabeth. That is what kings do. We cannot have brutal rogue elements roaming the land."

"Send patrols," she said. "Don't leave me."

"I'm not going anywhere for today," he said. "Or tomorrow."

"That's not good enough! You must promise me you will not leave for…" her eyes darted about as she tried to think of a number, "a hundred years!"

"A hundred years? I think you will grow tired of me if I never leave in a hundred years."

"I will never grow tired of you," she said, lying back down to press her soft body against his.

He pressed kisses to her cheeks, her nose, her mouth, gently reassuring her that he loved her and did not want to leave her. But it was not enough. Hot tears glistened in her eyes at the mere prospect of not having him by her side. Milo marveled at the power of the bond which seemed to have formed between them all so quickly.

"Remember a little while ago, you would gladly have thrown me from the top of this tower," he said in gentle, teasing tones. "When we are all healed from this, the feelings will not be so bad. I am sorry you had to see me hurt. I wish I could take that image from your mind and replace it with a happier one."

"I am sad you were hurt, but not that I saw it," she said, surprising him. "Now I know what the world is truly like. Now I know the castle is the only safe place for any of us to be."

Milo's heart broke a little as he realized he had been part of a loss of innocence. Elizabeth's father had kept her locked away in the tower for much of her life and as a result she had been sheltered from the realities of war and of the cold nature of the world. She had likely never seen the results of violence until she saw him.

"The world is not always so cruel," he said. "You must know that too. There is much good to be had."

"Thus far an old woman has poisoned me, and an old man has tortured you."

"Well, that is true," Milo admitted. "But there are good things besides that…"

"Like what?"

"Well, there are sunsets and sunrises…"

"I can see both of those things from the tower," she pointed out pragmatically.

"There is the thrill of the open plain, of seeing new vistas, new worlds. New people…"

"Some of whom tie you to a tree…"

"Most people do not," Milo reassured her, pressing kisses to her temple as his hand roamed the length of her back in soothing strokes. "You have seen little of the world, and what you have seen has scared you, but there is much to enjoy outside the castle walls."

"Will you show me?" She looked up at him hopefully, her green eyes brimming with a wholehearted trust that made his chest swell with a masculine pride and sense of protection. Thanks to his foolishly allowing himself to be captured, she had seen some of the worst of the world. He was determined that she would see the beauty of it too.

"I will," he said, taking her by the hand. "Come, Elizabeth. We are going to see the stars as you have never seen them before."

• • • • • • •

Excited and a little afraid, Elizabeth followed in Milo's wake. She smiled up at him he led her from her chamber to the landing that they would descend from the tower. Heavy footsteps were ascending in the opposite direction.

Milo and Elizabeth stood at the top of the stairs as Ragnar tramped past. He was utterly filthy, his hair matted against his head, his beard plastered to his chin. He reeked of sweat and dirt and something more animal in scent. It was all Elizabeth could do not to hold her nose as he approached.

He had never looked more like a barbarian than he did in that moment. Had she not known him well, she would have been utterly terrified by such an apparition. He nodded to the pair of them as he ascended the final step. His shoulders were bowed as if he were exhausted from some great feat. Elizabeth noted that his axe was strapped to his back, but the blade had been damaged. A great chunk had come out from the middle of it.

"Gusig will not trouble us again." Ragnar said the words flatly. "I need a bath."

Elizabeth's eyes widened as she took in the full weight of his words. He was not covered in dirt. He was covered in dried blood. A tremor of horror raced through her body and she pressed close to Milo as fear made her throat close over.

There was a strange look on his face, something oddly blank and removed. She did not see the man she had known. Instead he was an empty vessel of muscle, bone... and blood.

Having said his piece, Ragnar continued on his way without another word. He did not turn back to look at either Elizabeth or Milo as he walked to the bathing chamber with a heavy, tired step.

Elizabeth looked up at Milo. "Did he...?"

Milo's expression was grim. "We are going to look at the stars."

"But..."

"Stars," Milo said firmly.

Elizabeth could not help but notice that although Ragnar claimed to have dispatched Milo's enemy, Milo did not seem particularly pleased about it. If anything, he seemed annoyed. The ways of men were quite unfathomable to her.

"But..."

Milo turned to her. "I promised you beauty," he said. "And you shall have it."

She smiled a little at his resolve. He was not thinking of Gusig, or of Ragnar. His mind was on her and her alone. He took her by the hand once more and led her down the stairs without another word. Elizabeth fell silent too, feeling solemn, confused, and a little sad. Was this to be her life now? A steady procession of men bloodied in either victory or defeat?

They rode out together, flanked in the mid-distance by a small platoon of Milo's soldiers. Elizabeth was still much concerned by what she had seen, but Milo did not seem inclined to talk about it. He took her to a hillock a few miles outside the city, set out his cape upon the grass, and drew her down next to him.

"You will see many things in your life," he said, his arm wrapped around her to keep her close and warm against his body. "Some of them will be terrifying. Others will be beautiful beyond imagination. Look."

She looked upward and saw what he was pointing at, a great array of stars splashed in a milky ribbon across the dark sky. The moon was overshadowed by the beauty of the bright lights that were in grand array. She had seen the stars before, of course, from the window of her room. But she had never seen them with Ammerdale sitting among them, the silhouetted castle seeming picturesque and calm. It was difficult to believe that it had recently been the scene of a double invasion. It was difficult to believe how much turmoil had taken place across the silver hills and plains laid out below them.

"Pain passes, horror fades. All that remains is beauty," Milo intoned. "No matter what happens. No matter what you should see or experience, remember that."

She looked at him with wonder in her eyes. He was a king and a warrior, but he had a poet's heart. His intelligence was his greatest weapon, she was sure of that. Many other men would have been impossibly shamed by having been seen in a state of defeat, but Milo accepted it as part of the natural course of things.

"Sometimes we shall win. Others we shall lose. I cannot promise you an easy life, princess. But that is not what life is. It is not easy. All anyone can do is live it. Do you understand what I am saying?"

"You are saying you will not hide in the tower with me forever," Elizabeth said. "And Ragnar would never consider it. You are saying that if I love you, I must also live with the pain of losing you one day."

"Perhaps, perhaps not," Milo said with a rakish smile. "Ragnar and I are inordinately good at what we do. One king may fall where two stay strong. I am saying that win, lose, or fall, we can endure." He tipped her face up to his and kissed her gently. "You must be brave, princess. We must all be."

His kiss filled some part of her soul, made her body fizz and her head spin with excitement. She turned toward him, her thighs parting, her dress riding up over her hips as Milo freed his manhood and pressed it to her dewy lower lips.

Elizabeth let out a soft sigh of satisfaction as Milo filled her with a gentleness that made her spirit sing. They made long, languid love there upon the hillock, Elizabeth free of the dark castle in the distance and the mental shackles that had tied her to it her entire life. She was safe, not within walls, but in the arms of a man whose passion triumphed over defeat.

# CHAPTER ELEVEN

In the very early hours of the morning, Milo returned to the castle with a sleeping Elizabeth in his arms. She was so beautiful in her repose and as he settled her into bed, he felt an overwhelming sense of love and desire that almost transcended the unpleasantness that was about to ensue with Ragnar.

The barbarian was asleep in a nearby bedchamber that he had claimed for his own. Milo had no compunction about waking him up with a boot to his bed.

Ragnar opened one eye. Even with just one eye open he seemed gruff and grumpy. As well he might be after a day of mayhem and likely, murder.

"So you killed him," Milo said flatly. "Gusig."

Ragnar opened his other eye and fixed Milo with the full force of his barbarian gaze. "You do not seem pleased."

"I will never have my revenge. Already the stories are spreading of how you strode into his encampment and cleaved his skull with your axe. The bards have been strumming and humming all night long. I heard them in the great hall practicing their songs as I came up here."

"That is a bad thing, I take it."

"They are singing of me too," Milo said. "They are

calling me 'little Milo.'"

Ragnar guffawed.

"You think this amusing?"

"I think you should pay less attention to the bards," Ragnar said. "I did what had to be done."

"And you did it alone, to prove your strength."

"I did not do it alone," Ragnar replied. "I had a contingent of men with me. Twenty-one men, in fact—and a spy who was paid handsomely to tell us of Gusig's location. I was not the only one who bloodied his blade."

"The bards are singing you did it alone."

"The bards sing whatever they feel like singing," Ragnar sighed. "I did what I needed to do. A man attacked us. I settled the score. You would do the same had I been attacked."

It occurred to Milo that he was being petulant. More petulant than Elizabeth, at times, which was quite an achievement in its own right. He looked at the barbarian king and allowed another feeling to enter his heart—gratitude.

Milo put his hand on Ragnar's shoulder. "Thank you," he said. "For coming for me. For avenging me. I have never in all my years had anyone who would do that for me. I apologize for my earlier rudeness, for leaving it to the bards to sing your praises. I have just spent the night teaching Elizabeth to accept the slings and arrows of fortune and here I am throwing your efforts in your face..."

"Save the formal speeches," Ragnar said with a grin. "Your thanks is enough. And even that isn't needed. It was my pleasure to gut the man. I had thought of nothing else since we found you tied to that tree. The bards will sing and our enemies will think twice before moving against us again."

"I warrant they will," Milo agreed grimly. "It was a matter of vengeance, then."

"It was a matter of vengeance and justice." Ragnar sat up and fixed Milo with a look full of uncharacteristic passion. "We have a legacy, Lionheart. Ours is a kingdom of three. We may already have sons and daughters growing in Elizabeth's belly. I will never allow one of our own to be touched without furious retribution, and it is well the world knows that."

"I pledge the same," Milo said. "You have my sword. You have my soul."

"Good," Ragnar said, lying back down. "And now I will have my sleep."

• • • • • • •

The beef between Milo and Ragnar was easily settled, but matters between Elizabeth and Ragnar were more complex. Unlike Milo, who expressed his concerns bluntly, Elizabeth kept her to herself, preferring to smile sweetly and leave the room every time Ragnar entered. After several days of such behavior, Ragnar began to notice the pattern. A few more days, and he remarked upon it to Milo.

"That princess…" he said as Elizabeth once more made her apologies and found a pressing need to be elsewhere.

"Yes?" Milo replied.

"She is frightened of me," Ragnar said. "She has been hiding in your skirts since she saw me after my battle with Gusig."

"She is perhaps a little frightened," Milo agreed.

"She has not been content to be in the same room as me for a week. She hides from me."

"Have you spoken to her about it?"

"I have bade her good morning and good evening."

Milo fixed him with a direct look. "But have you talked to her about the night she saw you coated in the entrails of another man?"

"…No."

"Perhaps you should," Milo suggested.

"Talking," Ragnar said. "That is what I must do, you think?"

Milo smiled his wicked smile, full of intellect and humor. "You are such a barbarian," he teased Ragnar good-naturedly. "How else are you going to know what is in her mind and heart unless you use your words?"

"I am not accustomed to this," Ragnar said, his brows drawing down into a frown that contained no small measure of warning for Milo. "Your help is more appreciated than your jests."

"You do not need my help. You need your tongue," Milo said with a laugh. "She is in her chamber, I believe. Go to her, King Ragnar. Give the bards something else to sing about."

"I will give you something to sing about," Ragnar growled, shaking his fist at Milo.

Milo grinned as Ragnar went to deal with the princess. Though they had been lovers for some time, they were yet to have what Milo would have regarded as a 'proper conversation.' Ragnar was not typically a man of many words, but he knew he would have to find some if Elizabeth were to learn to trust him. Ragnar knew Milo shared much more in common with Elizabeth than he did. They were royalty of traditional lineages. They understood one another as a result of a lifetime of common experiences. But Ragnar was a barbarian, and Elizabeth was a refined princess. There was a gap between them that seemed of late to have widened to a chasm.

Ragnar knocked on the door of her chamber and waited until her lilting feminine voice bade him enter.

"Hello, Elizabeth," he said as he stepped into her chamber and shut the door behind him. She was sitting in her favorite place in the window seat and she did not turn to look at him as he came in.

"Hello," Elizabeth said shyly, avoiding meeting his gaze.

He walked over and sat in the chair near the window. Still she did not look at him. She parted her lips as if to speak, and unfurled her legs in a motion that strongly suggested she was about to make yet another escape from his presence.

"Come here, princess," he said. When she did not immediately obey, he reached out, wrapped his large hand around her slim wrist, and drew her gently toward him until she was settled upon his knee. "We need to talk," he said, wrapping one arm about her waist to keep her in place.

"We do?" She looked at him under her eyelashes with an expression that revealed a mixture of awe and respect and a little bit of fear as the large barbarian held her close.

"Have I frightened you?"

She squirmed with the effort it took to find an answer to the question that wasn't a simple affirmative.

"I frightened you," he said, saying it for her. "I am sorry."

"You were different that night," she finally said. "I almost didn't recognize you."

"I was filthy," Ragnar agreed. "But…"

"No, you were different in your face. In your eyes," she explained. "You felt like a different person."

"Battle can do that to a man," Ragnar tried to explain. "I am sorry I frightened you. Milo says I should have avoided seeing you, and I think he was right. I forget sometimes that protecting you means protecting you from war."

"You are very used to it," she said. "It made me think how many times you must have looked like that as your barbarian horde came rising from the south. How many of my father's armies have fallen to you, the fearsome Ragnar…" She trailed off, a little shiver running through her body.

"I was born to war," Ragnar admitted. "I saw my first battle at the end of my seventh year."

Her eyes widened with shock and disbelief. "No army recruits a soldier so young!"

"I was not recruited into an army. I was forced to defend my village. I did so with a kitchen knife and a pot lid shield, standing alongside the men."

• • • • • • •

There was a gravity in Ragnar's voice, a heaviness that touched Elizabeth's heart. She had some sense that this was a story he had not told before, and that she would likely not hear it again. Though he was strong and imposing, in that moment she saw a shadow of the small boy he must once have been, and her heart went out to him.

"The village men did not make you hide?"

"I refused to hide," Ragnar said. "Even then I was a bloody minded creature. They let me stand with them, knowing full well that if they were to lose, I would be done for anyway. They were brutal times, Elizabeth. Lawless lands. I swore then that I would make sure any place I lived would be safe from those who did cruel harm."

"And so you became a barbarian king," she said. "And conquered my kingdom."

"No man becomes what he wants to be without also becoming that which he hates," Ragnar said, speaking with a heavy heart. "In making my lands safe, I became the one who was feared. Seeing that fear in your eyes..." He broke off. "That is not what I want."

"I was afraid," she admitted. "I think, perhaps, I still am. It is natural to fear a powerful man. But it is also natural to love him."

A smile broke across Ragnar's face. "I do not think you have said you love me before."

"I do not think I have either," she said, smiling until his lips met hers in a passionate kiss that demanded the full use of her tongue and took the power of speech away. She felt his hands begin to roam over her body in gentle caresses that belied his physical power. With Ragnar, she always felt dwarfed, but he was taking such tender care of her that it was no cause for concern. Fear had fled under the massaging of his tongue and the gentle play of his hands over the curves of her body.

For long minutes they kissed, slowly experiencing a new

connection that was not purely based on conquest or domination, but on a longing they both shared. Elizabeth turned ever more toward him, until she was straddling him, her thighs on either side of his legs as she gave herself to the barbarian who had avenged the evil that threatened her.

"I know I have done more good than evil in this world," Ragnar breathed against her lips. "Because the gods have granted me the right to hold you in my arms."

Elizabeth felt her eyes welling with tears of emotion. Ragnar did not often speak of his feelings, but his words, though gruff, were rich with love. She could see his desire, his care, his utter devotion in his eyes as she gazed up at him and knew beyond a shadow of a doubt that this man would protect her with every breath in his body. He was devoted beyond measure.

She let her head rest against his chest and heard his heart beating inside the muscular walls, a steady, reassuring sound.

"I am sorry I was avoiding you," she said in a small voice. "That was cruel of me. I should have hailed you as a hero, not treated you as a leper."

"There is no shame in being afraid of something frightening," Ragnar said, comforting her with a tight embrace.

"I'm glad you are on my side," she said with a little smile. "I would not want to find myself on the wrong side of you."

"The only thing you need to worry about is finding yourself over my knee," Ragnar replied, patting her bottom lightly. "I'll give my all to keep you safe, Elizabeth. Sometimes that means I will do things that are frightening. But I will always care for you. I will always be on your side."

"Always?"

"Always," he promised.

# CHAPTER TWELVE

With their domestic affairs seemingly settled, Ragnar and Milo were free to turn their attention to the running of the kingdom. Combining three individual kingdoms into one great land was no easy matter. Many were fractious and there was the risk of conflict at every old border. Sometimes that conflict would creep into the city in the form of an assassin, and for that reason, as well as her previous dubious purchases, Elizabeth was forbidden from leaving the castle without escort. The market was especially off-limits, a fact she often bemoaned at length until either Milo or Ragnar threatened to thrash her so that she might have something else to complain about.

The kings held weekly court to attend to the concerns of their new city and kingdom. Most of the time those who came to petition them were lords or high merchants, but one day they found themselves confronted with a rather tatty and thoroughly terrified peasant who came forward, clutching his hat in his hands and trembling visibly.

"My lieges," he said, bowing so low his nose almost touched the floor. He stayed there, trembling until Milo called for him to rise and say his piece, which he did, albeit with a great deal of stammering reluctance.

"I speak for the Ammerdale traders. Since the coming of your graces, we have been more prosperous than ever, but prosperity has bought those who would take advantage of us. Robbers roam the market, growing bolder by the day. We fear for our safety, and the safety of our customers."

"Fear not," Ragnar said. "We will triple the guard."

"And pay a bounty for anyone who catches a thief or robber," Milo added.

"Thank you, my kings," the trader said with an audible sigh of relief. "It's just, we have been so worried about Princess Elizabeth. She does not seem to know the dangers. When we tell her, she simply laughs. We fear her innocence may lead to some harm…"

Ragnar and Milo exchanged looks. "Elizabeth is at the market?" Ragnar asked the question.

"Without guards?" Milo added.

The trader began to tremble all the more. "I have said too much…"

"You have not said enough," Ragnar growled, leaning forward from his throne with a scowl. "Tell us what Elizabeth has been doing in the market. Do not leave a single detail out."

• • • • • • •

Suffice to say, court was ended prematurely that day as both kings excused themselves from the castle and made their way down to Ammerdale City. It was not difficult to find Elizabeth in the market, for her feminine form was surrounded by a ring of traders, all of whom were offering her their finest goods in the hopes of receiving some of the gold she was dispensing from a large pouch at her waist.

"Brazen," Milo noted. "Utterly without any fear whatsoever. One would think she would give half a thought to the consequences of her disobedience…"

"We have spoiled her," Ragnar replied. "And now we must un-spoil her."

He strode toward the princess, pushing through vendors as if they weren't even there. The crowd parted for him and Milo, though Elizabeth was so caught up in the joys of commerce that she did not notice either of the kings approaching until they were towering over her.

"Uh…" She looked up at them, holding a green emerald necklace that sparkled prettily in the sun.

"Put that down," Milo said firmly.

To the surprise of both kings, Elizabeth refused to do so.

"I want it," she replied. "I have already given the coin for it. It is mine."

"You are not supposed to be here," Ragnar growled from the other side of her. "Where is your guard?"

"I don't need a guard," she said. "These are my people. They would not hurt me."

"We told you that you were not to come out without one. That is what matters, our orders." Milo knew he was wasting his breath, but he could see that Ragnar was about to take matters into his hands, and it would go better for Elizabeth if she could manage just a sliver of apology for her disobedience.

"You may take your orders," she said in rather pert tones, loud enough for the wider crowd to hear her. "And you may put them in your posteriors."

There was a collective gasp at her rudeness and sheer bravery. Milo could only shake his head at her, incredulous at how brazen she was being. It occurred to him that she seemed to want to be punished. Things had been quiet of late; perhaps she was missing a royal sting in her rear.

Ragnar did not bother to question her motives. He took hold of the impudent princess, grabbed a nearby stallholder's stool and sat upon it, hauling the princess over his thighs without further warning.

"No! You cannot do this to me! Not here!" Her cry went up immediately.

But he could do it. In fact, he was already doing it. Her

skirts were tossed up over her back, baring the royal posterior.

"Ragnar! No! Put my skirts down at once!" There was real desperation in her tone, but it had not lost any of its imperious aspect either.

"You have forgotten who you are speaking to," Ragnar growled. "You do not give me orders, princess." His hand came down across her pale cheeks, sparking them bright pink in the shape of his palm.

"You should be protecting me! Not humiliating me in front of these peasants! You said you would be on my side. You said you would always be on my side!"

Milo almost admired her ability to stick to her story, though it was not earning her any favors or mercy where Ragnar was concerned. He held her firm and spanked her bottom hard with steady strokes that offered little respite. "I am on your side. And right now, the side of you that needs tending to is your backside."

Milo let out a snort. Ragnar was not usually one for wordplay. A little ripple of amusement went through the crowd in response to his jest, which seemed to have gone right over Elizabeth's head.

"But I am the queen!"

"You remain a princess," Ragnar corrected her. "A spoiled, naughty little princess who is going to pay for her misdeeds."

The small crowd that had initially witnessed Elizabeth's undoing was growing into a larger one as people all around the market gathered to see what the commotion was. When they saw that it was the princess being punished, the news rippled out among them and drew still more people.

"People are watching!" Elizabeth cried out to Ragnar.

"You didn't mind people watching when you were being rude," Ragnar growled. "You shouldn't mind now that they are seeing you be punished for it."

"Milo! Help!" She made a desperate appeal to Milo, but he merely shook his head as he stood there, his arms folded over his chest.

Elizabeth's bare red bottom was fast becoming just as rosy as the apples in a nearby stall. Her bouncing made her cheeks jiggle in an appealing manner that drew lascivious gazes from soldiers and common men alike. She was enjoying very little in the way of modesty, but she had forfeited that.

"We gave you an order for your own good!" Milo took over the job of lecturing as Ragnar's palm beat a steady tattoo on her bottom. "We did not confine you to the tower, or the castle. You were allowed free rein as long as you took a guard with you. And what did you do? Flout our rules and make a mockery of our law in the marketplace."

Perhaps the spanking was wearing at her petulant resistance. Perhaps Milo's stinging words had gotten through to her. Perhaps both factors together were responsible for Elizabeth's surrender.

"I'm sorry!" Tears began to well and then fall from Elizabeth's eyes, but tears and simple apologies were not nearly enough. Her impudence and petulance upon being caught disobeying them and putting herself in danger yet again were not dismissed by a few swats to her bottom.

Elizabeth sobbed, but Ragnar spanked on until her bottom turned a deep red hue, her cries became ever more desperate and the mood of the crowd began to turn and the onlookers started to call for clemency.

"She's had enough!"

"Let 'er go!"

"What say you?" Milo lifted his voice. "This young woman has disobeyed the kings of this land and put you all in danger by bringing unguarded riches to the market that may attract robbers and thieves. Do you think a warm bottom is enough to teach her?"

There was a rabble of replies, some in the affirmative, some in the negative. Milo saw the effect of the response upon Elizabeth regardless. She was thoroughly shamed by the public nature of her punishment and wanted nothing more than for it to end.

Ragnar let her stand up, but not before giving her another sound swat to her swollen cheeks. "Apologize," he growled.

"I am sorry," Elizabeth said tearfully. "For everything."

Taking pity on her at last, Milo swung her up and over his shoulder, carrying her from the marketplace with her still bare bottom held high for all to see. Ragnar stayed behind, giving orders to the guards and the stallholders as to what must happen if Elizabeth were to make another unaccompanied appearance.

Elizabeth sniffled all the way back to the castle, and did not stop her feminine complaints until Milo put her on her own feet in her chamber. There, a different Elizabeth emerged almost immediately. He noticed the moment he put her down that she had a rather peevish expression on her pretty face. It boded ill even before she opened her mouth.

"That was awful," she sighed, rubbing her bottom in an exaggerated fashion. "Ragnar can be so unreasonable. I am glad you are not so given to brutish acts of so-called discipline."

It was quite a revelation to Milo that Elizabeth had not in fact come close to learning her lesson. She had given such a convincing performance down in the marketplace and made the crowd believe she was truly penitent. But the truth was, blushing bottom aside, she wasn't sorry at all. Not one little bit.

"I shan't sit for days," she sighed, kneeling by her window. "Fortunately, I purchased a lovely silk cushion from a merchant just a few days ago." She flashed a roguish grin at Milo, seeming to dare him to take her to task.

"Come here," Milo said, crooking his finger.

His tone must have cued her to the presence of yet more trouble, for her green eyes went wide. "But... I have been punished. And forgiven. We are done."

"Oh, we are far from done, princess."

"But the peasants… they said I had enough…"

"We decide when you have learned your lesson," Milo replied. "Ragnar and I. And I, for one, do not think you have learned it at all. I would never have thought after all that has passed that you would so blatantly flout our orders."

"You would never have thought I could do such a thing? Then you have not thought very deeply," Elizabeth replied pertly.

Milo's brow rose. Not only was she unrepentant, she was rude. It was most surprising, but perhaps not unexpected. For the first time since the castle had been captured, she was in a settled state. She had likely always been a spoiled little brat, but there was far too much chaos in the castle to notice just how pronounced it was.

"You think it wise to speak in such a fashion?" He asked the question in a tone that Elizabeth would have recognized as a dangerous one if she were not spending so much time being an unrepentant little witch.

"Ragnar isn't here," she said. "I am in no danger."

She was taunting him. And that was a mistake.

"So you think Ragnar is the only one capable of disciplining you thoroughly." Milo chuckled darkly. "You do not often press me, princess," he said. "But you have pressed me far enough to see just how very wrong you are."

He crossed the room, took her about the waist, and tossed her upon the bed before tearing her dress from her with one vigorous snatch of his fist. The silk fabric parted quite easily at the seams, baring her soft curves to his burning gaze. Elizabeth let out a cry of shock as she found herself suddenly naked beneath a much more commanding man than she had expected to deal with.

He looked down at her not with anger in his eyes, but with a dominant determination that made her quiver. Milo watched as a flash of realization passed over her face. She had forgotten during the course of their association that Milo was every inch the king Ragnar was, a fine fighter, a scholar and a gentleman. In the midst of the attempted coup that had made him its primary victim, she had made the mistake of taking his kindness for weakness and his intelligent, refined demeanor for yet more weakness.

What she had failed to take into account was his penchant for invention and his steel determination to achieve his aims. It was he who had implemented the chastity belt that had gone by the wayside so quickly in the aftermath of her psychedelic misbehavior. He had something new prepared for her now.

"I have had some instruments for you," he said. "Something I thought I might use for your pleasure, but will work just as well as a means of discipline."

Milo was prepared for this moment. He had put aside a number of implements and tools about the place, either for future pleasure or punishment. It was the work of a moment to open a dresser drawer and draw out two thick phalluses carved in wood. One was longer and slightly thicker than the other, and the smaller had a flared base, but either could have adorned a man had it been made of flesh.

"Ah," Elizabeth said. "From your cock collection. I imagine it holds a great many pieces."

He smirked at her. "You recover remarkably well for a young lady who was sobbing and begging for leniency not half an hour ago. On your knees, princess. Reach back and spread those ruby red cheeks for me."

His order made her blush, just as he had intended for her to.

"I will not ask you twice, Elizabeth."

He watched as she struggled with her desire to continue to give him cheek, and the desire to save her own cheeks from further spanking. She had utterly destroyed any chance of not having her bottom warmed again, however; the sheer nerve of the girl was impressive.

When he said nothing, she began to slide into position, lifting her ass up as her cheek pressed against the linen of the bed. Her feminine fingers went back to her hot cheeks, still broadly marked with Ragnar's palm in pink lines that stood against the pale tone of her skin.

Milo had some preparation to do before he began his phase of the punishment, but he left her in that position as he moved things around. She began to make impatient noises, and to let her cheeks move back together.

"Spread them, Elizabeth!" He snapped the words harshly enough to make her obey him instantly. She spread her punished bottom cheeks and held her two holes for him in the most vulnerable way possible—the wet slit of her fiery pussy and the tight pink star above it.

He took the larger of the two toys and began to draw the tip of it along the length of her slit. She was quite wet, as he had expected her to be. As much as she might blush and resist obedience, her body responded to his domination.

"Remember, you could have had a much easier path, Elizabeth," he said as he teased her soaking pussy. "If you had some respect for me, or anybody for that fact. You have been spoiled, princess. You will not be after this."

She let out a little moan as he started to push the flared head of the toy toward the opening of her body. He knew it felt like pleasure. It would not feel that way for long.

"Look in the mirror," he ordered. "I want you to see this as well as feel it."

She turned her head to see her bottom displayed in the shiny surface, the pink inner lips of her pussy already spreading around the tip of the toy.

· · · · · · ·

Being publicly thrashed had been embarrassing, but what Milo was doing took her notion of embarrassment to a new level. If he had simply fucked her, she would have been caught up in his passion. Instead she was the one losing control as the thick carved phallus slid slowly into her pussy, twisting slowly with every motion of his wrist. Her juices made the polished shaft gleam as he worked it into her body.

Finally, he slid the toy all the way into her cunt—and then he left it there. Elizabeth let out a little whimper as she watched the thick end of the polished toy sit an inch or so out of her pussy, her lips gripping it with pulsing motions she could feel to the very core of her.

Before she could fully adjust to the toy in her pussy, the tip of the second wood cock was pushed against a much more sensitive little hole—the bud of her bottom.

"No!" she moaned.

"Yes," Milo growled back. He pushed the thick head of it a little more firmly, making the resistant muscle give way. Only once her bottom had shown some submission did he produce an oily lubricating lotion, dabbed against her anus. It was not a lot, but it was enough to ease the passage of the thick, hard intrusion as it began to press and stretch all the more, teasing the tight ring of muscle with demanding little strokes.

"You're going to have both your holes filled," Milo informed her, his refined tones making the crude words all the more embarrassing. "Both tight, naughty little orifices stretched for me."

Elizabeth felt her pussy clench around the phallus as the second toy began to breach her bottom properly, making its way past the tight ring of muscle and sinking an inch or so inside her. She let out a gasp, her fingers clutching at the sheets as she felt herself stretched impossibly wide, the barrier between her two channels thin enough that she could feel the phallus in her bottom rubbing against the one in her cunt.

It took quite some time for him to work the second one fully inside her. Her bottom was very tight and her body was resistant, but Milo did not give up. Even when it seemed that her little holes could take no more, he simply applied more oil and continued working the phallus deeper into her bottom.

She was whimpering and squirming, her hips dancing a

slow, desperate gyration, which perhaps helped a little. Complicit in her own punishment, Elizabeth was still caught against the bed, her bright red face and hair pressed against the sheets, a little puddle of wetness where she had gasped and moaned so many times.

"You're drooling with pleasure," he said, noticing it. "At both ends."

Elizabeth shut her eyes to save herself from the sight of her heated ass being plugged and filled, but he soon bade her open them again.

"I want you to see yourself, princess," he said. "And next time you think of disobedience, or any form of inappropriate behavior, I want you to remember how it was to have your hot little bottom lifted high for me as I fill it."

Her cunt clenched again, her clit tingling with excitement. He was drawing every bit of physical and emotional sensation out of the situation, letting nothing pass unfelt or unremarked upon.

Elizabeth squealed as his fingers swatted around her rather full pussy and bottom, his fingers slapping her spread lips, her stretched bottom hole. He had her totally in thrall around the two phalluses, and though she was filled, it was not enough to satisfy. She needed her greedy little clit rubbed hard in order to orgasm, but he would not do it. Occasionally his punishing fingers would land across the naughty bud, sending a shock through her loins, but not providing near the stimulation necessary for climax.

She was utterly undone, desperate for orgasm and denied it at every turn.

"Please," she begged. "Fuck me."

"I will fuck you when I wish," Milo replied, his very calmness seeming cruel as he once more denied her what she so desperately wanted. "You haven't earned my cock, princess. You spent far too much time being recalcitrant and rebellious, and invested far too much energy in disobedience."

"I am sorry!"

"You said you were sorry when Ragnar thrashed you in the marketplace, and that was a lie," Milo said. "Why should I believe you now?"

"Because I am sorry!"

"Not good enough, princess," he said, tutting. "I want to hear a truly heartfelt apology from you. I want to know beyond a shadow of a doubt that you pledge your obedience to me and Ragnar."

His words stung more than his palm did, though that too was still raining slaps on the most sensitive parts of her anatomy.

"You disappointed me today," he continued with the lecture. "And now here I am punishing you like the naughty wench you are. You spank the same as any woman, Elizabeth. Being a princess does not stop your bottom from turning red, does it?"

"No!" she gasped yet again. "Milo, truly! I am sorry! With all my heart!"

He pulled the phallus from her pussy in one smooth stroke. She felt bereft of it, but not for long. Milo positioned himself on the bed behind her, his hips lined up with hers, his erection pointed directly at the very core of her melting desire.

"Please," she begged. "Please!"

There was real desperation in her tone, for his cock, for his forgiveness, for everything he was and everything he could give her... and finally, it worked. Finally, his cock sank inside her, his hardness stretching her pussy wider than the wooden toy had. Elizabeth let out a primal cry as he wrapped his hand in her long red hair and eased her head back so she was arched against him, her well spanked bottom pulling hard against his thrusting hips as he began to fuck her vigorously and without mercy.

Her breasts bounced beneath her, her lips parted in a continuous feminine wail of desire, pleasure, and an undeniable tinge of pain as her stinging cheeks were slapped over and over by his hard hips. The phallus in her bottom kept that tight hole stretched wide, yet shifted and moved inside her too, providing yet more inescapable stimulation as he plunged inside her with deep, commanding strokes.

She thought she was at the very limit of her erotic capacity—and then the barbarian arrived.

"Well." Ragnar's deep voice cut through her high-pitched wails of pleasure as he stepped into the room. "Look at you, princess."

She could see herself in the mirror, red hair stuck to her face in wisps that were caught by the sweat trickling down her cheeks. Her eyes were gleaming with arousal, bright with desire. Her body was flushed and covered in beads of exertion. Milo had put her through all her paces and still he was urging her on to even greater heights.

Milo slapped her bottom and plunged his cock in and out of her completely one more time. She moaned as his hard rod left her clenching pussy bereft of any stimulation. He was toying with her, and she felt it keenly.

"This little witch wasn't quite as sorry as she seemed, would you believe it?"

"I would believe it a thousand times over," Ragnar growled, a dark smile on his face as he stripped his clothing from his body and walked toward her, his cock hardening with every step he took. "I just told the stallholders that they will receive three hundred gold pieces for reporting you to me if they see you without a guard. I have already paid the peasant who told us first," he said, taking her by the chin. "Open your mouth."

Elizabeth obeyed without thinking, her lips parting wide enough for Ragnar's cock to slide into her panting, moaning mouth. He began to thrust over her tongue, using the lips of her face much like he used the lips between her thighs.

"Three hundred gold pieces," he growled down at her. "And you will work for every one of those pieces, I promise you that."

She looked up at him, her mouth full of his hardness as Milo continued to fill her with stroke after stroke. The toy in her bottom kept her anus occupied and her senses reeling as she was moved back and forth between Ragnar and Milo stroke after stroke in a relentless motion. She was caught between them in an erotic prison that satisfied as much as it tormented.

She thought the sensations were as great as they could be, then Ragnar reached over her body, took the base of the anal toy in his fingers and began to thrust it in time with the thrusts of his hips. Now all three of her tight little orifices were being played and she was utterly overwhelmed with the lust of the kings who owned her. She could smell the musk of their desires, especially upon Ragnar's cock as she took it deeper and deeper into her mouth.

His hard flesh pulsed against her tongue. She could feel that he was not far from orgasm already. The sight of her spread around Milo and the toy, her wanton body finally in submission to a higher authority was almost too much for him to resist.

The earlier sternness and disappointment had melted in both of them. Now it was pure lust and the animal domination of two alphas bringing their woman into line. With the submission of her body, the unfettered expression of her lust, Elizabeth had earned more than forgiveness... she had earned climax.

Milo's hands were clamped tight on her waist as he pistoned his cock in and out of her at an ever-increasing rate. The pounding made the plug in her bottom bounce with every movement, driving her closer to coming, but she did not attain it until Milo's hand slid beneath her, his fingers found her punished clit and began to strum there. It was as if he had the power to command her physical form at will. With the touch of his fingers on that wet little bud, Elizabeth's body sang out in one great note of pleasure as her exhausted loins fired in one great symphony of erotic sensation that went crashing through her tender frame.

This was not an orgasm. This was the fulfilling of a dream, the falling into place of a thousand disparate pieces.

This was the end of the beginning, the place in which her mind could no longer fight what her body had always known.

She belonged to these men.

As she moaned and writhed in complete climactic abandon, Ragnar and Milo thrust themselves as deep inside her as they could go. Two loud shouts of climax emanated from their throats and shortly thereafter two streams of semen flowed into her belly and womb. She tasted Ragnar's cum as it splashed over her tongue and trickled down her throat, her impulse to swallow all too natural. Her pussy was performing much the same action, her hungry walls clenching to draw Milo's cum ever deeper inside her.

A sweeping wave of post-coital ecstasy passed over her, putting a blissful smile on her face. Her body was soaked with her sweat, her ass was burning from the spanking she had been given in the marketplace, her bottom was still filled with the anal toy. There was no doubt in Elizabeth's mind that she was utterly, totally owned—and that being owned was the highest state of grace there could be for a princess such as she.

Milo pulled his cock from her and eased her down on the bed, leaving the toy inside her bottom for the moment. She curled up with her back against his body as Ragnar joined them, facing her, kissing her lips where his seed was still lingering about her mouth.

"We love you, Elizabeth," Milo murmured against the back of her head. "We love you enough that the next time you misbehave, you will be plugged and wear the chastity belt for a month."

She bit her lower lip, avoiding a mischievous response that she knew would not serve her, and instead kissed Ragnar again, tasting the barbarian and his cum. Behind her, Milo was rubbing her bottom gently in a motion that not only soothed, but served to make the toy gyrate slowly inside her tightest cavity. The punishment was not quite over. It would probably never entirely be over, Elizabeth thought to herself. She would remain naughty and they would remain stern, and together it would all work out.

Between the two of them, they had taken her to a place of physical and mental submission from which she would never fully return. Her spirit was not broken; far from it, her spirit was soaring as she cuddled between the two kings who commanded every inch of her.

She had never wanted the trinkets from the marketplace. She had wanted to know, beyond a shadow of a doubt that Ragnar and Milo were capable of taking care of her no matter what. She had needed to know that no matter what impulse rose in her, they would keep her safe, even from herself.

Now she knew beyond a shadow of a doubt that Milo and Ragnar acted in accord with one another. They had begun as enemies, and their alliance had been tenuous at times, but she was sure now that it was as strong as it needed to be. Through betrayals and beatings and bards singing songs to taunt one or the other, they had come through it all. Together, their strength was magnified and she would not likely escape their attentions for long should she tend toward chaos again. The kingdom was in safe hands, and so was she.

Finally, after many months of turmoil, after a life waiting for the man of her dreams, her Prince Charming, Elizabeth settled between her two kings and fell into the sweetest, deepest sleep of all.

# EPILOGUE

"And this portrait is Elizabeth of Ammerdale and the kings of Ammerdale."

A group of graduate students stared at the portrait being shown to them by the wizened curator of antiquities in the Modern Ammerdale Museum for the arts, located in the old Ammerdale castle. In the portrait a beautiful redheaded woman with remarkably graceful features and eyes that contained a hint of mischief stood between two men, one broad and dark with scars on his powerful features, the other elegant and blond with a cocky tilt to his head. It was a formal portrait, but there was an undeniable intimacy to the way the figures were positioned closely to one another, both men having one arm wound around the princess, gazing at her with an intensity of adoration that made a few of the students rather jealous.

"Was it common for women to have two husbands then?"

"Not at all," the curator said. "Elizabeth was a unique royal figure in many regards. Her contributions to history extend far beyond her progeny. She was the first to introduce a system of taxation and commerce that…"

"How many offspring did she have?" Another student

127

broke in with the question before the curator could go off on a tangent about taxation and other dry subjects.

"Elizabeth bore seven heirs in total," the curator said. "Popular legend has it that three were blond girls known as the princesses of the north; three were dark-haired girls, known as the daughters of the south; and the very youngest one was a redheaded boy…"

"Ragnar the Red?" one of the students guessed.

"Precisely. The king who took the east and west and unified the isles as we know them today." The curator waved a hand at the intimate trio. "These are the people whose unorthodox love affair not only created the first stable alliance between kingdoms, but laid the groundwork for the modern political landscape…"

The students soon moved on to the next picture, but Elizabeth and her lovers remained smiling over Castle Ammerdale, and all who lived in the sprawling city below.

# THE END

Printed in Great Britain
by Amazon